GUARDING HARPER

BROTHERHOOD PROTECTORS WORLD

TEAM WOLF
BOOK ONE

DESIREE HOLT

Twisted Page Press LLC

Thank you

To those who help me labor, who support me in the toughest hours, who encourage me, who brighten my day and make it all worthwhile: Margie Hager who reads it all in its rawest form; to Steven Horwitz, without a doubt the best most supportive son in the world; to my daughters Suzanne Hurst and Amy Nease for their unflagging encouragement and support. And to Maria Connor, world's best assistant, without whom there would be no Desiree Holt.

To Elle James, for inviting me into her World and sharing her characters with me.

Last but far from least, to my wonderful readers who take this journey with me every day and who have made writing these books a blessing.

Montana D-Force (#3)

Cowboy D-Force (#4)

Montana Ranger (#5)

Montana Dog Soldier (#6)

Montana SEAL Daddy (#7)

Montana Ranger's Wedding Vow (#8)

Montana SEAL Undercover Daddy (#9)

Cape Cod SEAL Rescue (#10)

Montana SEAL Friendly Fire (#11)

Montana SEAL's Mail-Order Bride (#12)

SEAL Justice (#13)

Ranger Creed (#14)

Delta Force Rescue (#15)

Dog Days of Christmas (#16)

Montana Rescue (#17)

Montana Ranger Returns (#18)

GUARDING HARPER

TEAM WOLF BOOK 1

New York Times & USA Today
Bestselling Author

Desiree Holt

PROLOGUE

Gabe Walker regarded the five men gathered in Hank Patterson's kitchen, along with Hank himself and Stone Jacobs, the Brotherhood Protectors leader who had reached out to them. They all had the same look of the hardened warrior, the take-no-prisoners attitude, which was good. They weren't here for playtime. The work Stone had hinted at needed men like him and his teammates.

Gabe had gone into the military right out of college, after his parents passed away, and there was no longer a place for him on the Texas ranch where they'd worked. Disillusioned by the manner of the drawdown in Afghanistan, they'd all – he and his team - left Fort Drum, headquarters for the Tenth Mountain Division, not reupping in the Army. Since then they'd been putting their skills to use in a security and consulting service. Their motto for their First Brigade Combat Team was "Find a way or make one," and they'd kept that in place.

When Stone and Hank had approached them, they'd been told a big plus was the fact they'd been working in the Adirondacks, which gave them plenty of experience in the mountains. His team had kept their motto as they created a place for themselves in civilian society. They were all hardened military men. No job was too tough for them.

Gabe was aware that Stone himself had made a major change when Hank Patterson reached out to him. Hank had built a vast security organization that took on the most challenging jobs and could operate where other agencies could not. Stone owed Hank big time for getting him out of a dangerous situation overseas before Hank left the military. He'd made sure the men knew why Brotherhood Protectors was so important to him. Folding his own one-man operation into Brotherhood Protectors seemed like the most productive thing to do. Especially when Hank told him he wanted this part of the organization based in Yellowstone. It was a win/win because Stone's father owned a lodge in Yellowstone, and he was very familiar with both the territory and the turmoil going on in that area.

When he reached out to the men with his proposal, they'd all been interested. After all, new challenges were what they were about. The more challenging the better. He'd told them when he approached them that the fact they'd all been working in the Adirondacks would make an easy transition for what he had in mind.

Gabe shifted his attention to the man leaning against the kitchen counter. The one outlier in their group. Alex "Ridge" Ridgely. He had been part of their team at Fort Drum and had the hardened, experienced persona they needed. He was slightly older than the others, but that was because he had enlisted later. The men on Gabe's team had welcomed Ridge's experience, and he was a steadying influence.

He also was dedicated to wildlife preservation, which meant this might be right up his alley. He'd at least been interested enough, after two meetings, to show up today and listen to the entire proposition. And the others were glad to see him at least entertaining the offer.

And now, here they were, waiting for the rest of the details that would shape their team.

"Anyone need a coffee refill before we get started?" Hank asked.

They all topped off the liquid in their mugs before taking their seats at the table again, all except Ridge who returned to his spot against the counter. Still reserving judgment, Gabe thought.

"You all know how Hank Patterson and I met,"

Stone began. "He saved my ass in a big way when we were both still in the military, and I've owed him big time ever since then."

"Not so," Hank interrupted. "You've paid it back in spades." He grinned. "But I'm happy to have you obligated to me."

"I know we've explained Brotherhood Protectors to you," Stone went on, "but just a little refresher here. Hank started it when a situation arose with Sadie, now his wife, and just grew from there. We handle kidnappings, illegal aliens, anything that comes up. No job is too challenging. "

"So you told us," Justice Kane said. "But what specifically do you have in mind? I'm sure you don't expect us to stand around taking target practice until a job comes along that we like."

Stone grinned. "There won't be much time for hanging around, trust me."

"You said something when we first met about establishing us in Yellowstone, but you never went into the reason why."

"Wolves," Stone told them. "That dwindling species."

"I understand it's becoming a bigger and bigger problem." Nate "Edge" Edgerton sat on one of the barstools, his black German shepherd, Pierce, lounged but alert at his feet.

Stone nodded. "Park rangers eliminated the last wolves in Yellowstone National Park in the 1920s, but they were reintroduced in 1995. The project has been lauded as a conservation success story. The internationally acclaimed Yellowstone Wolf Project oversees research and monitoring of wolves in Yellowstone."

"But exactly what does that have to do with us?" Wade Fielding asked.

"Good question. There seems to be all kinds of crap going on where wolves are concerned in Yellowstone. Despite the organization's and individual efforts, it's become more than local law enforcement or wildlife officers can handle. People are hunting wolves for sport, for profit, or because they interfere with their lifestyle. This is especially true of the ranchers who don't want to work with the wildlife officers and licensed volunteers."

"You mean they're poaching?" Justice asked.

"Worse. In many instances, they draw them out of the areas fenced for them to roam freely then kill them. They can sell the pelts for high dollars on the black market. And that's only part of it. Some ranchers are trapping them and letting them loose on a rival's ranch, so they can attack the cattle and put the rancher out of business."

"Shit." Gabe Walker had been rocked back in his chair, listening carefully to what Stone had to say. He had a vague idea of what was happening with wolves in the area, but this, what Stone had just told them, turned his stomach.

"Indeed," Hank agreed. "The project and the wildlife officers make a concerted effort to ensure the wolves stay inside the designated area for them.. But once they leave the park, they're fair game. And there are plenty of assholes who take advantage of that fact."

"I'm still curious as to what role we're supposed to play," Wade said.

"We have men releasing wolves from the park area to trap and kill. Moving them to other ranches to kill cattle. Using them as attack animals to achieve a purpose. And then there are those who just don't like the wolves period and will do anything to get rid of them. We've had two civilians shot and killed during wolf incidents, and it can only get worse if someone doesn't put a stop to it."

"Shit." Justice let out a slow whistle.

"And that's not all," Stone went on. "We have a well-run wolf sanctuary here that's constantly under attack. Harper Young, who runs it, works her ass off but is constantly coming under fire. People want to shut her down, kill her wolves, destroy her property. You have no idea how vicious people can be when it comes to the preservation of wildlife."

"I'm familiar with it." Ridge pushed himself away from the counter. "My clients I take on excursions talk about it now and then. And it's a big topic in the wildlife community."

Stone turned to him. "So you'd be interested in becoming part of this operation?"

"I'm interested in finding out exactly what it is you want us to do."

"Fair enough." Stone nodded. "We'll take this on a case-by-case situation. If you guys are all in on this, my father has room to house you at his lodge in West Yellowstone until you find other lodgings you might prefer. When you aren't on an assignment, we'd like you to study everything you can about the wolf situation at Yellowstone. Talk to people. Get a feel for where trouble might be brewing."

"Is there enough to keep us busy full time?" Ridge asked.

Hank snorted a laugh. "More than. In fact, we've got a situation with Harper Young right now that needs immediate attention. We need someone on the premises, protecting her, scoping out the situation, sniffing around for gossip, and finding out who wants to shut down the sanctuary before they kill her and her wolves. If everyone is in, I'll do a blind draw and assign someone to this."

Gabe nodded, as did the other men.

"But I'd like to see this in operation before I take an assignment," Ridge added.

"Fair enough," Stone told him. "Okay." He grabbed a coffee mug filled with slips of paper from the counter. "All your names are in here. Hank will pull one, and tag, you're it."

Hank closed his eyes, reached in, and pulled out one of the slips.

"Well, well, Gabe. It looks like you're first up at bat."

Gabe smiled. "Good. I'm hungry for action."

"I have to warn you. Even though she did ask for help, Harper Young is one feisty woman, so watch yourself. She doesn't take orders easily."

Gabe chuckled. "Then I guess I'd better be sure not to give any."

"And keep in touch. I want to know anything and everything that happens that is the least out of the ordinary."

"Done. Let's just hope my being there will make anyone think twice about messing with her again."

"My dad's expecting the rest of you," Stone told the others. "Rooms are on the house. You just need to cover your meals. I have directions to his place, so you can settle in." He grabbed a box from the counter and placed it on the table. "Cell phones. We'll program them now, and they will only be used for Brotherhood Protectors business."

They spent the next few minutes setting up the phones and making sure they each had all the numbers. Then Stone texted them the directions to his father's lodge.

"I'm going to head on over to the sanctuary,"

Gabe said. "Introduce myself and get the lay of the land."

"Good." Stone nodded. "I told Harper someone would probably be by today."

"Can I pitch my tent there? I'll feel a lot more comfortable doing it, and it means I can be right there all the time."

"Sure. Harper might even be happy about it. Means she has protection right there, although she'd like to think she can handle everything herself."

"Great. How about giving her a heads-up I'm on my way?"

"Just as soon as I get everyone else out of here. She's had a couple of incidents that have made her really edgy, so this will be a good thing." He scratched his head. "You know, people like Harper and the other wolf conservationists are doing really good work. Maintaining a species of wildlife that was nearly extinct. They've created sanctuaries, conduct tours so people get the real story of wolves, make sure there are vets available when needed. But some asshole always thinks he has the right to destroy it. Not to mention the anonymous threats she's gotten."

"Damn." Gabe shook his head. "Okay, I'll get all the information from her and get her to give me a tour of the place and introduce me to anyone she thinks I should be in contact with."

"And if situations arise where you need other members of the team," Hank told him, "just reach out. That's what this is all about."

Five minutes later, with directions programmed into his cell, Gabe was on his way, wondering just what the hell lay ahead of him with wolves and poachers and possibly murderers.

CHAPTER 1

HARPER YOUNG MADE notes in the daily logbook she kept then closed out the computer file. It had been another exhausting day, riding the preserve in the four-wheeler someone had been kind enough to donate, and checking on the latest wolves she'd managed to rescue. Each wore an electronic collar with its own identifier which made it easier to check on them. She gave thanks that in the last week only one wolf had disappeared. Probably because she was also installing electronic sensors on some of the fencing, so she knew if someone tried to bust through.

She was exhausted protecting her gray wolves from marauders. There were the poachers who wanted the fur to sell on the black market. There were the ranchers who fought her on a daily basis because they didn't want her wolves anywhere near their cattle. She kept trying to tell them that if they left the damn fences alone, they wouldn't have to worry about it. But they just wanted the animals gone. Period. And would do anything to make that happen. Then there were those who wanted them for the sport of hunting and left the carcasses to be destroyed by other predators. Once a week, at least, she checked the radio-controlled collars each wolf wore to make sure they were all alive and well.

When she'd first come to work for Jim Haggerty at Yellowstone Wolf Preserve, she'd been appalled at the total disregard for the animals she found in the area. The wolf was such a majestic animal. Despite the reference to gray wolves, they were actually timber wolves that came in all colors—from almost completely white to solid back. It pissed her off when the state legislature raised the number of wolves that could be killed during hunting season. She was working hard with a group to get that changed again.

She'd learned so much from Jim: catching the wolves, caging them to place the collars, checking their health, making sure they weren't hurt. She'd learned how not to frighten them and how to ease them back into the wild. Every experience had ramped up her commitment to them.

She leaned back in her chair and let out a sigh. Little did she know, when she'd gotten her degree in wildlife management, how fascinated she would become with what she was doing. When she graduated, she'd done a search for sanctuaries hiring people, and this had one appealed to her. She'd visited Yellowstone a few times, been impressed with the majesty of the place, and sent in her application.

"Don't get too excited," Jim Haggerty had warned her. "It's a lot of work, a lot of politics, and just us."

That was the damn truth. And now, since Jim's heart attack, it was just her and two college students who worked part-time. And Andy Gregory, the vet who was a godsend.

One of the perks was the living quarters that came with the job, a well-constructed and well-furnished cabin. She and Jim had shared it until his heart attack sent him to live with his daughter, but Harper didn't mind being by herself. It was certainly convenient, and the best part? Rent free.

If not for the overeager poachers and the ranchers determined to get rid of her one way or the other, it would be an ideal situation. Lately, she'd had some close calls, one late at night when she'd decided to check out what was going on had been way too close for comfort, so she'd taken to carrying a gun. Stone Jacobs had set up a target range for her away from where the wolves usually roamed and worked with her until he deemed her proficient enough she wouldn't shoot herself instead of the bad guys.

Too bad someone had been miserable enough to spoil what was one of her favorite times of year at Yellowstone. September ushered in fall, the wildflowers changing colors, the conifers like lodgepole pine and white bark pine standing like majestic guardians, and shrubs like juniper and sagebrush decked out in their dark fall coats. There were large stands of trees, stretches of shrubs and bushes punctuated with open spaces.

Usually, the trees and shrubs soothed her as she rode the preserve, especially as the end of summer approached, but lately, she'd been sleeping poorly, always on the alert for the sound of gunshots. After the night she'd seen someone on horseback, who had obviously jumped the fence and was hunting with a shotgun, and someone else had actually taken a shot at the wolves, her sleep had grown very sporadic.

"Have you gone to the Yellowstone Wildlife Sanctuary people?" Stone asked when she told him.

"Many times," she said, "but there is only so much they can do. And some of the poachers and hunters have a lot of financial and political clout, which makes moving on them very difficult. The sheriff told me they need proof of what it might be before they can actually do anything."

"Well, I can offer some help, at least for protection. I don't like the fact that someone took a shot at you."

"Neither do I."

"Okay, then. I told you about Brotherhood Protectors and the group I started here as part of it. You're their first assignment. A man named Gabe Walker is assigned to you and will be here twenty-four seven."

Harper frowned, thinking.

"Is he going to share my cabin with me?" The thought of sharing her space with a stranger left her uneasy.

Stone's laugh sounded over the phone. "No, don't worry. He'll pitch a tent. After all those assignments in Afghanistan, a cabin would be too comfortable for him."

Harper sighed. "I hate to think of him sleeping outside like that. It gets cold here at night. I don't want him to freeze to death."

"Don't worry. He's slept in every extreme of temperature there is. He'll be fine."

"What's he like, this Gabe Walker?"

"Well, he's a Texan, first of all. I'd trust my life to a Texan anytime. Second, he was part of a team stationed at Fort Drum, headquarters for the Army 10th Mountain Division. Hank Patterson, chief honcho of Brotherhood Protectors, and I felt this would give them the best skillset to translate into work at Yellowstone. The motto for the 1st

Brigade Combat Team is, "Find a way or make one."

She snorted. "Sounds like just what I need here. A smart-ass Texan."

"That's why I assigned him," he told her. "Nothing fazes him. I fact, he should be arriving in" —he paused—"about another hour. Want me to come by for introductions?"

"I think I can handle it, but thanks."

"Okay. He'll check in with me after he gets settled."

"Thanks, Stone. I really, really appreciate it."

"What are friends for, right? Catch you later."

Harper checked her watch. Nearly an hour had passed since Stone left, which meant Gabe Walker would be arriving any time now. In fact, as the thought flew into her brain, she heard the sound of an approaching vehicle, tires on the gravel in the parking lot, and the closing of a truck door. There was glass in the upper part of the door to the office, so she could always see who was approaching, but she wasn't sure she was ready for what she saw right now.

The man who opened the door and walked in was about six feet tall, every inch visible muscle even through his Henley sweater and his faded jeans. Dark hair hung to just below his chin, framing a chiseled face with a scruff beard. Inky lashes enhanced onyx eyes that seemed to see right through her. It was all topped off with a well-worn ball cap that said 1st Brigade Combat Team. Masculine toughness rolled off him in waves, along with an invisible current of electricity that zapped all her lady parts.

The impact was enough to make her long-sleeping hormones suddenly awaken with a vengeance and start screaming. *Damn! What did you send me, Stone?* This was not good. She hadn't had a date since she began working at the preserve, and she hadn't missed it. But apparently her body did, and how inconvenient was that? Damn again.

I only hope his protective skills are as strong as the hot sexy vibe oozing from him.

"Afternoon." His voice was a deep, husky baritone that shockingly sent shivers through her and made her pulse race. And was that a Texas drawl? What the hell? And holy shit. A Texas accent.

"You must be Gabe Walker." Thank the lord she managed to keep her voice even and objective.

"At your service, and I do mean that."

Yep, all Texas for sure.

He held out his hand, and when she placed hers in it, he clasped it with strength and an air of toughness. Unexpected tingles raced up her arm, and heat warmed her system. What on earth? He was here to protect her. Nothing else. Besides, she didn't have time for any personal activities. She was too busy saving her wolves. She needed to get her act together. She didn't have time for this, anyway.

"Harper Young." She gave a nervous giggle. *Giggle? Really? Get your shit together.* "But then you know that, right?"

"Yes, ma'am. Stone gave me a complete briefing. I understand you're being besieged by unfriendlies who aren't happy with the wolves."

"You could certainly say that."

"Like I said, Stone gave me the basics, but I was hoping we could tour the preserve while you fill in the details."

"No problem. Let me get the ATV out of the shed, and we'll get going. But don't you want to set up your living quarters first?"

His laugh held the same rough edge as his voice. "I could do it in my sleep. It can wait. I'd rather get fixed in my mind what the deal is here."

"Okay, then. Let's do it."

She took her handgun from her desk drawer, checked it carefully, and shoved it into her pocket.

"You won't need that with me," he told her.

"I'd carry it if you were Jesse James. Humor me."

She could tell he wasn't happy, but he dropped his objections.

As she walked out of the office to the lean-to where she kept the ATV, her slightly battered Jeep, and the van she used for tours, she saw that his truck certainly suited his image—a dually pickup with reinforced bumpers and a raised cover on the bed. She bet the window glass was bulletproof, too. This man was definitely ready for anything.

He unlocked the cab and removed a rifle as well as a handgun. "I like to be prepared," he told her. "Like you."

She watched him as he climbed into the ATV, the muscles in his thighs and ass making her mouth water.

Damn, Harper!

She needed to get her shit together or this would all fall apart. She hadn't been attracted to a man in forever, not even her sexy friend Stone Jacobs. Now wasn't the time to start.

"Here we go, then." She placed the gun between them on the seat. Then she cranked the engine on the four-wheeler and backed it out onto the gravel.

"You handle that like it's nothing," Gabe commented.

"Experience." She pulled out onto the rough terrain. "Let me give you a little background on my babies. Gray wolves are the largest of the members of the canid family. The Yellowstone wolves were almost eliminated at one point, but the population has been growing for a while. When they were taken off the endangered species list, it seemed to become open season, even though there is a limited hunting time, and no hunting is allowed within the sanctuary."

"But you have people who don't give a shit." He glanced over at her as they bounced along the bumpy terrain. "Right?"

"You said it. They not only want to get rid of the wolves, they want to get rid of me. They see me as a big nuisance."

"I imagine so. We'll have to show them how wrong they are."

She snorted a laugh. "I'm not even sure that's possible. A lot of these men have great power and money and influence. That's how they get the rules changed and how their poaching and all is ignored."

"They haven't met us yet," he told her. "Okay, let's see what we got here."

They rode along the miles of fencing that delineated the preserve, the land on both sides broken by thick stands of trees and rocky outcroppings. Gabe sat next to her in what she realized was a deceptively relaxed position, but she knew he was taking everything in. She showed him some spots where people had clipped the wire and then tried to leave the strands loosely connected. That way they could let the wolves out whenever they wanted and entice them onto land where they were fair game. She explained that the quotas for wolves outside the park had been raised, but that didn't eliminate the problem. The hunters believed all wolves were fair game, and it didn't stop poachers from sneaking wolves out of the park to hunt them.

"I wish we had the money to have permanent patrols," she told Gabe. "At least the poachers and those looking to kill for other reasons would be put on notice."

"How did you get involved with this, anyway?" Gabe asked.

"I majored in wildlife management," she told him. "And I fell in love with the wolf. Yellowstone wolves are a species unto themselves—magnificent, majestic, regal. I saw the ad for a job here, and the rest, as they say, is history."

"Tell me more about the ranchers. For instance…" He pointed to a sprawling ranch house off in the distance, visible behind fencing in a section of rolling flatland.

"Ed Culhane owns the Four Diamond Ranch. It's been in his family for several generations, growing bigger each time his grandfather then his father drove neighboring ranchers off their land. The Culhanes used every dirty trick in the book to amass what is now ten thousand acres. One of the four largest in Yellowstone."

"Well damn." Gabe stared past the fencing.

"Ed Culhane's the most dangerous—to me—of all the ranchers," Harper told him. "He thinks he has the clout to do whatever he wants, which I think would include killing me if he thought he could get away with it. I ride the fence line every day, and I am always finding places where he's cut the wires then loosely reconnected them. I report him, but he denies it. And no one wants to go up against his money and power. I worry even more because one of his ranch hands is a former sniper."

"Yeah?" Gabe glanced at her. "So am I, and I'll bet my skills against his anytime."

Just hearing him say that gave her an unexpected feeling of security. At least she had that on her side.

Thank you, Stone, for this.

"Does he ever shoot wolves from his property onto the preserve?"

Harper shook her head. "No. He'd have to find a way to remove the carcass. It's easier to steal the wolves out of here and shoot them outside the fence line."

Gabe didn't comment, but Harper saw him studying the boundaries even more intently as they drove along. As they wove in and out of the trees and skirted the clusters of shrubs, she pointed out three more ranches whose lot lines touched the preserve at some point. She also indicated a dirt road that others used to get close enough to cut fencing and release the wolves.

"One of the things my students do each day is check for breaks in the fence line, like I told you. The only places they stay away from are where there are thick clusters of trees on both sides of the fence. I have concertina wire on the top to discourage people. My kids repair any cuts or breaks other than those caused by natural wear and tear , but it is a never-ending battle."

"I asked Stone, but I'm asking you, too. Doesn't the US Fish and Wildlife organization help protect them?"

"Not the way I'm supposed to. They have a large responsibility, and this is just a small part of it." She bit back what she really wanted to say. "Some wolves roam outside the fencing, but not enough to satisfy either poachers or ranchers."

As shadows grew longer, some of the wolves came out of their hiding places and raced across the ground in pairs and threes. Once in a while, a solo wolf burst onto the scene. When Gabe lifted his gun, Harper rested her hand on his.

"They're used to me," she told him. "Don't bother them, and they won't bother you."

They had reached the end of one line of fencing and, as they turned the corner, Harper spotted a man on horseback watching them from a thick stand of trees. It was hard to miss the rifle lying across his thighs.

"One of your unfriendlies?" Gabe asked.

"Definitely. That's Ed Culhane's spread, and I believe that's his foreman, Don Bracken. Ed has him keeping an eye on what goes on here. That cluster of trees is a good place for them to observe. They're pretty much concealed but close enough to shoot if they want to. I imagine there'll be some heated discussion when he tells Ed about the new face at the preserve. They might start plotting for a way to get rid of you."

"How many times have they shot at you instead of a wolf?" he asked.

"Only once, so far," she told him.

"Once is one time too many," he told her.

"They make sure I know they are watching me. I'm sure they think that just their presence will frighten me away. Make me give up my job. Besides, I don't think they were actually trying to hit me."

"You don't strike me as someone who caves."

She laughed. "You can't be and do this job. It makes me angry that these jackasses think having money gives them the right to get away with anything." She paused. "Even murder, I guess."

"The damn law enforcement should look into it," he growled.

"And do what? I don't have shell casings. I can't really spare the time to look through the grass for bullets, and it's nothing but my word against whoever. I'm working to get both state and federal help, but that takes time. And again, it's all politics."

She waited while Gabe studied the land outside the wire fencing. It was pretty much open for the cattle to graze, but it was dotted here and there with clusters of trees like the one where they'd spotted the man on horseback. Harper looked carefully at each one they passed, searching for other men, ranch hands, or the ranchers themselves, waiting, rifle in hand, for their opportunities.

They had driven for another ten minutes when she stopped the ATV and pointed to a rocky outcropping. A midnight-black wolf stood in a majestic stance on the highest point.

Gabe tightened his grip on his rifle, and she touched his hand with hers.

"We're good. The wolves are used to me by this time. And the Wolf Project people know we're tracking and monitoring them. We want electronic collars on all of them, so we know if one is missing. Their peak activity is at dawn and dusk, which means before long more of them will be coming out of the shallow caves they sleep in or the shelters of the rocky outcroppings. And they don't need to kill me for food because there is enough variety of wildlife to satisfy them. All you have to do is relax, and we'll ease by him."

"I noticed there are scattered chain link pens that we passed. Are they all over the preserve?"

Harper nodded. "They're what I release the wolves into when we get permission to move more onto the property. Also to place the electronic collars. The overhang and skirt discourage the wolves from digging or climbing over the fencing. Each pen has a small holding area to move the wolf into for medical treatment or collaring."

"This is quite the operation," Gabe commented.

"It is. It's a lot more than fenced property with wolves running wild. Especially with poachers and killers battling each other to get rid of the animals."

"You get a lot of poachers?"

"Not as many as we used to. Jim Haggerty, my old boss, made it difficult for them. He drove the perimeter enough with his rifle to let people know poaching wasn't going to be tolerated. Mostly our trouble comes from the ranchers who just want us and the wolves gone."

"Do you get close to the wolves?"

"Oh, sure. We work to get them used to us and to get them to know we won't hurt them. Some of them are still skittish, but we bring them along little by little. This is a safe place for them, which is why the shooting pisses me off so much." She nudged him gently with her elbow. "Maybe we'll get you to make friends with them."

Gabe laughed. "We'll see. I promise nothing."

They sat quietly for a moment while she gave him time to study the wolf and the area surrounding it. Then she shifted gears and eased slowly forward. They continued to ride over the acres of the preserve, Harper wanting to give Gabe a big visual picture of the place. Glancing now and then at Gabe, she couldn't help noticing that despite his outwardly relaxed position, he was alert and studying everything around them. They spotted some of the other wildlife and even managed to see a couple of wolves doing their thing, but they didn't come close to the ATV.

"You're right. They were magnificent animals," he told her. "But I think I'll enjoy them from a distance."

The sun had begun its descent by the time they reached the office again.

"So, that's the preserve." She waved her hand. "What you see is pretty much what you get."

"The landscape is gorgeous," he told her. "Those trees and the shrubs, all wearing their late summer colors. This is a gorgeous place to work. Sure beats all the sand we pounded in 'Stan and the freezing cold of the Hindu Kush. But don't you get bored out here?"

"Would *you*?"

He grinned. "Fair enough. And now I'm going to set up my tent while there's still light to see what I'm doing."

"I told Stone you're more than welcome to the other bedroom behind the office. No one's used it since my boss retired and I took over."

"That's okay. I like sleeping with nature. Plus, I've got plenty of comforts." He shrugged. "I'm used to it."

Tingles wriggled through her body. Damn! How was she going to survive this, especially since Culhane, the other ranchers and the poachers seemed to be stepping up their game. She didn't think they'd actually kill her, but they could create a situation where the state of Montana closed the preserve, and that would just suck.

"I bought a couple of steaks when I knew you were coming," she told Gabe. "Dinner in an hour okay for you?"

"You don't have to go to any trouble."

Harper waved him off. "I have to eat, too, so no problem. It might be nice to have company for a meal for a change."

His sexy mouth curved in a hint of a smile.

"See you in an hour."

CHAPTER 2

Ed Culhane poured an inch of bourbon into his coffee, sat back in his chair, and lifted his booted feet to the small table in front of him. He sipped the coffee, savoring the taste as it slid down his throat. Nothing better to end the day than a fine bourdon, and this was one of the finest. Over the rim of his mug, he eyed the man sprawled in one of the other chairs.

He and Frank Winslow had been friends since they were kids, growing up on neighboring ranches, competing together in rodeos and generally raising hell when they could get away with it. One thing about being part of a family with a shit ton of money—you could get away with damn near anything.

Except getting rid of the fucking wolf preserve.

You'd think between him and his close friends

they had enough money to buy off any government entity, but apparently it didn't work like that. And he was fucking sick and tired of hearing how the government weenie "had a responsibility to the people."

He'd love to get rid of all the wolf lovers, take down that fence, and hunt whenever the mood struck him. They could charge the idiot poachers a fee to hunt on their lands and control the situation so he and his friends had the best pickings.

"My foreman tells me the bitch has someone new on her property," he told Frank. "Some guy who's not from around here."

"Yeah?" Frank took a sip of his coffee.

"Yeah. He saw her giving the guy a tour of the preserve late today"

"Wonder where the hell he came from and why we don't know? There's nothing that goes on here that we don't know about."

Ed snorted. "I'd like to think so, but apparently she's got a few tricks up her sleeve."

"Too bad getting rid of her would cause more trouble than it's worth," Frank mused. "We'd be better off doing away with a couple of the poachers. Tell people it was an accident. That ought to calm them down for a while."

"We have to be smart about it. That Yellowstone Wolf Project researches and monitors the wolves, and they're well known in nature and education circles. Like I said, it has to look like an accident and disrupt the operation of the preserve."

"What if they just hire someone else?" Frank asked.

"We have to point out how dangerous the work is and make sure anyone interested in the job is well aware of that."

"We can always blame it on those asshole poachers," Frank pointed out.

"Yeah, I'd rather find a way to scare them off for good. We ought to call a meeting with Don Bracken, your foreman, and put a plan together for that. If not for that public road that cuts through our ranches, it wouldn't be a problem. Let's get everyone together for dinner and discuss it."

"Good idea. We need to do it soon, though. And definitely need to find out who that guy is riding around in the ATV with Harper Young."

"You call the guys. I'll reach out about the stranger. Let's get a move on."

STONE JACOBS REFILLED his coffee mug and carried it out to the porch along with his cell. Early evening was always his favorite part of the day, neither too hot nor too cold, most times with a little breeze. Gabe Walker had checked in with his cell phone to let him know he was at the Yellowstone Wolf Preserve, had set up his tent and equipment, and was ready to go.

"You all settled with Harper?" Hank Patterson's voice rang clear over the cell line.

"As settled as possible." Stone barked a short laugh. "She's a prickly thing, isn't she?"

"She needs to be, in her situation," Hank pointed out. "She can't ever let her guard down, and she can't relax enough to overlook something that might come back to bite her in the ass."

"Gabe will make sure she's protected," Stone assured him. "He's the best one for the job."

"How's that?"

"He has a sister who's a lot like her."

Hank burst into laughter. "Leave it to you to come up with the ideal match. Okay, keep me in the loop, and let me know if you need anything."

Stone disconnected the call then punched in the number for Gabe.

"Can you talk?" he asked when the man answered.

"Yes. Harper's working late in her office, and I'm outside away from the building. Stone, you told me about the ranchers, but did you know about the poachers, too?

"Unfortunately, yes. I'd like you to see if there's any connection between the ranchers and the poachers. Like maybe the asshole ranchers are using those idiots to get rid of Harper."

"I had that thought myself. Maybe spotting for them. She took me on a tour of the preserve, and there was a guy hiding in a copse of trees along one side. Harper said it was one of the hands from the Culhane ranch, but he could be gathering information and making sure these other jackasses have it."

"You need to find a way to sound things out in town. Maybe when the part-timers are at work at the preserve, so at no time is Harper alone."

"I thought of that. I'll work it out. But I promise you this. She is 100 percent safe with me."

"That's why you got this assignment," Stone agreed. "Okay, regular check-ins and all that. We're still sorting out assignments for everyone, so don't be afraid to ask for help."

"So far so good," Gabe assured him. "But I'll definitely shout out if things change."

GABE DISCONNECTED the call and went to get the rest of his equipment from his truck. Harper Young had surprised him. He'd expected a tough female with rough edges and an attitude. After all, who else would play with wolves?

Harper was a total surprise. Tall and slender, she didn't look like she could wrestle a humming-bird until he shook hands with her and was shocked at the strength of her grip. Then he'd noticed the flex of muscles in her forearms and the strength of her hand clasp. Streaky blonde hair was tied back in a long ponytail, and when she walked, he could see the working of the muscles in her legs.

Not to mention her ass.

Damn, Gabe!

Get your head out of the gutter. You're supposed to be protecting this woman, not taking her to bed. Let's see some of that famed Walker control.

He gave himself a silent talking to as he rigged his tent and set out his equipment: sleeping bag, extra blanket, bottled water, the tiny battery-operated fridge among other things. Then he gathered stones to set up a ring for his campfire and stuck his coffee pot and cooking pan in the tent. He took a long look around, just to make sure he hadn't missed anything. Only the soft crunch of gravel and the squish of wild grass let him know Harper had come up behind him.

"You really do have this down to a science."

"Iraq and Afghanistan don't leave much time for anything but." He checked the stakes on the tent one more time.

"I wanted to tell you that there's a door to the bathroom in the office, and you're free to use it whenever you need."

He grinned. "You want to make sure I don't lose all the niceties of life?"

She actually blushed, surprising him. "It's pretty

rough out here, but you're doing me a huge favor, so I want to reciprocate where I can."

Ed Culhane and Frank Winslow had decided their coffee needed a little spicing up. The man they'd seen with Harper Young still baffled them. They had made some discreet phone calls to other ranchers and to the Yellowstone Wildlife office to see if anyone had any information they could give them, but all they drew were blanks.

"How the fuck does a total stranger just show up here, one no one knows anything about?" Ed frowned as he took a sip of his coffee. "Not even the wildlife guys."

"I don't like it," Frank growled. "We had a good thing going here. All we had to do was keep harassing the Wolf Preserve, and pretty soon she'd be gone. Cutting the fences keeps her busy repairing them, especially now that it's just her and a couple of high school kids. So, who is this guy who appeared out of thin air?"

"My foreman who saw him says he looks tough as nails. And he had a rifle on his lap while they were taking their tour of the preserve."

"We need to make some more calls. Someone has to know something."

"Any new groups moved in lately?" Ed asked. "Never mind. We've already asked ourselves that."

"Well, he's a big stumbling block," Frank pointed out. "But he can't have eyes everywhere. We won't have the freedom to do our stuff like we did before, though, until we get a better handle on him. We'll never know if he's watching."

"I was hoping to get rid of the Young woman soon. Not kill her. Too many questions. Just put her out of commission."

"Yeah, well, we'd better figure out how to do it."

"I'm kind of hoping we can arrange a wolf attack," Ed mused. "That gets rid of her and the fucking wolves at the same time."

"That takes planning," Frank pointed out. "And we need to get a handle on this guy before we put anything in play. Let me nose around a little and see what I can find out. Meanwhile, a little mischief here and there won't hurt, and it might give us a better read on this guy."

Ed slapped the arm of his chair. "Let's do it. Figure out what might work, and I'll set it up."

"Meanwhile," Frank said, "let's send one of the men out riding the fences tonight and see if she and the guy are out patrolling. Maybe we can throw a little scare into them."

"I don't think he looks easy to scare," Ed commented.

"At least we can give him something to think

about before he gets too deep into whatever he's supposed to be doing here."

"Okay." Ed nodded. "Let's get it done."

HARPER SHUT down her computer and locked the office. She had worked much later than she usually did, but she needed something to take her mind off the man sitting just outside the office building. She wasn't used to being that overly conscious of a man, even before she got involved in the Yellowstone Wolf Preservation. She dated but never seriously. Once she connected with the wolves, it was even less. So what was it about Gabe Walker that made her so aware of him?

She thought about just going to bed early, but her mind wasn't ready to settle down yet, not with the masculine presence sitting outside her building. She needed to clear out her mind and stop fixating on this guy. She had serious problems here, and she didn't need to distract herself.

On the other hand, she should take advantage of every opportunity to show him what was happening at different hours of the day and night, especially the night. And tonight might be a good time. He could get a sense of what the wolves did at night, plus, she wasn't sure that ranch hand she'd spotted today watching them didn't have some-thing up his sleeve.

"You're welcome to come join me." The deep voice rumbled out of the darkness. "I can't offer you a chair, but you can bring a blanket if you like."

She stepped off the porch and walked to where he was sitting in front of the tent.

"Uh, thanks. The ground is fine for me." Taking a deep breath, she sat beside him, folding her legs and leaning back on her hands. She caught whiff of his masculine scent that had trickled past her nose earlier, some kind of woodsy cologne that only enhanced his masculinity. "You like sitting out here on the ground?"

"I did a lot of it over in the Middle East when we were staking out situations. Got used to it. I also wanted to get a sense of what happens here after sunset. Will it disturb anything if we take the ATV out at night?"

She shook her head. "I do it myself often enough to keep people on their toes. My boss taught me that."

"Good. Let's take a little ride."

Again, Harper noticed he took both his rifle and his handgun, checking to make sure both were loaded.

"Just being cautious," he told her. "Like before. 'Trust no one' is my motto."

"Probably a good one to have." She turned on

the engine and headed away from the office. "Shall I just ride the fence line?"

He nodded.

"You said the wolves won't bother me if I don't bother them. It's the two-legged animals on the land around us that concerns me."

"Okay, then."

She focused on her driving, scanning the areas on the other side of the fence, especially as they rode past Ed Culhane's ranch property. She kept an eye out for ranch hands, which was how, even in the dark, she spotted the man on horseback once again in a cluster of trees,

"Think he's planning to sleep out there on his horse?" Gabe joked, easing the tension.

"It's okay with me if he does. I'm used to it. As long as he keeps his gun holstered or against the saddle and doesn't come any closer."

"Do they really think they can get away with killing the wolves? I know there is a hunting season, but even that is limited."

Harper gave an unladylike snort. "As if they'd care. They just want to protect their cattle and maybe score some pelts while they're at it."

"Do the wolves attack the cattle a lot?"

She shook her head. "Only if they're provoked and outside the compound. If they'd leave us alone, we'd all be fine."

"Men like him don't believe in anything except

what they want. I've known too many of them in my life."

Harper made a turn at a corner of the fence and, in doing so, hit a submerged rock with her tire, tilting the ATV. She fell sideways against Gabe.

"Whoa, there." He righted the ATV easily and put his arm around her to steady her.

Heat shot through her at the feel of his muscular body against hers, enhanced by the brief touch of his fingers against the side of her breast.

Jesus, Harper. Get a grip.

"Sorry. Sometimes the rocks are hard to see at night." She righted herself in her seat. Then she glanced at Gabe, but in the dark it was hard to read his face. Had he felt the electric zing, too?

Then two things happened at the same time. They heard the howl of a wolf and the sharp crack of a rifle. Harper slammed her foot on the accelerator and headed at an angle away from the fence, toward a natural wall of rock where she stopped, catching her breath. The rocks were piled like a mini mountain and shielded them from anyone's eyes unless they had very powerful binoculars. She blew out a breath and leaned back in her seat.

"Shit," she swore. "That was close."

"He wasn't aiming to hit you," Gabe assured her.

"How exactly do you know?"

"Because I'm pretty damn sure if he was, he would have. I think he's just trying to throw you off your game. Scare you into doing something stupid. Which, by the way, I don't believe would work. He could have killed the wolf, though, but that would have been even worse. I'd have the park rangers and everyone involved with the wolves out here looking for bullets and trying to track the shooter. Guys like him are not very bright."

"You're right," she said at last, still gripping the wheel so her hands didn't shake. "He wasn't trying to hit me, but still… The ranchers can get away with a lot of things, but killing the person in charge of the wolf preserve would only bring down more trouble than they want to deal with."

"But they could make it impossible for you to do your job."

"And then what? If I leave, the organization will just hire someone else, although it could take some time, and this program could fall apart while that's happening."

Gabe shook his head. "That would be politically damaging. The problem is, people like these ranchers—and the poachers—don't believe that. They're probably convinced if they chase you away, they can bring pressure to bear to do away with everything."

Harper sighed. "Not happening. Too much pressure from the conservationist side. I have some pamphlets to give you about the program that will give you a better view of my side of the picture. I'll do it when we get back." She took a deep breath then exhaled in an attempt to settle her nerves. "All right, you up for a moonlight ride around the rest of the preserve?"

"Absolutely. But I have to ask, why aren't we calling the sheriff?" he wanted to know.

"Because it's just our word against that guy's, and he's got power behind him. And Ed Culhane financed his last campaign."

"That's another reason Stone sent me. We don't trust anyone but ourselves."

"Then…?"

"Then we just have to be more alert and make plans. That's why I'm glad we scoped out the preserve, so I have a visual of everything. And why I'm going to dig up info on your neighbors so we can get some leverage on them. Maybe find a way to exert pressure to get them to leave you alone."

"I'd sure be happy with that." She blew out a breath and rubbed her face with her palms. She was happy to see her hands weren't shaking.

"Want me to drive?" Gabe asked her.

"No, I'm good." She had to be. "I can't give up control on anything, or they'll get rid of me for sure. Here we go."

They drove slowly along the remainder of the perimeter then took a long diagonal line from one corner to another. The moon was higher in the sky now, and the landscape was more visible again.

They rode for quite a while before seeing any of the wolves, but then they spotted two of them running over a low pile of rocks. Moving as a team.

"Really magnificent animals," Gabe commented. "They don't seem too interested in us."

"They're not. Those two, for example, are probably mates out for a moonlight run or maybe looking for food. There's foxes, coyotes, bison, and elk—mostly elk—available for them, so they won't starve. In fact, look." She stopped the ATV and pointed.

In the distance, three wolves ran fast from an outcropping of rock to a cluster of trees. And beyond them, two elk stood tall against the horizon.

"Impressive," Gabe said. "Do you ever run into trouble with them?"

She shook her head. "I see them mostly when I'm tracking their habits. I don't bother them, and they don't bother me."

She put the ATV in gear again and moved forward. Another hour passed, without incident, before they headed back to the office area.

"I've seen enough for now," Gabe told her. "I wanted to get a good picture of the place at night in my head in case someone decides to pull some funny stuff."

"Mostly they just try to frighten me," she told

him "Like I said earlier, they're flexing their muscle, hoping to chase me away."

"We don't want them to get carried away," he reminded her. "And now I've got a pretty good picture of the layout in my brain, so I can do my own scouting and watching. I'll know better how to protect you."

"Thank you." She blew out a breath. "I hate to let these idiots scare me, but they're so stupid they might actually shoot me by mistake."

"We won't let that happen, and I feel I now have a better sense of this entire place in both daylight and dark. I want to do a little snooping in the area, too, and find out more about these ranchers. Tomorrow, I might take a ride over to Stone Jacobs' dad's place and pick his brains."

Harper parked the ATV in the lean-to, but she left the keys in it.

"In case you get the urge for a little trip," she teased then leaned against it.

She wasn't in any hurry to shut down, which irritated her. This was a business arrangement. Gabe was here for two reasons, to protect her and let the ranchers and poachers know he meant business. She had no business letting her long-buried emotions take over when she had work to do.

And she was sure Gabe felt the same.

But she had invited him for dinner…

"I'm going to put the steaks on now," she told him.

"I'm going to give Stone a call. Give me a holler when they're ready."

He walked off to the side a little, pulling his cell phone from his pocket and speaking in a low tone. Harper was sure it had to do with the shot at them. Stone would want to know right away. Would he decide things were escalating and insist she close up shop? If so, he'd have a fight on his hands.

He disconnected, and his words told her she was right.

"I reached out to Stone," he told her. "I wanted him to know you were still being used for target practice, although if that guy had wanted to hit you, he would have."

"They just think they can scare me away." She gave an unladylike snort. "Fat chance."

"I figured." He studied her for a moment. "You sure this is worth it? We could get you packed up and out of here in no time."

"And leave my wolves?" She gave him a shaky grin. "Not on your life."

"That's what I figured. Well, we need to be even more alert, and I need to ask Stone if he needs to send more people out."

"Okay, let me get dinner started. Being shot at didn't quite kill my hunger."

She busied herself grilling steak and potatoes

and throwing a salad together and, when it was ready, invited Gabe into the kitchen.

"This is good," he told her when he'd cleared his plate. "Thanks. It beats MREs all to hell."

"MREs?"

"Meals ready to eat. The staple when on a mission or assigned overseas away from regular food. So, thanks again."

She refused his help cleaning up. The kitchen wasn't really big enough for two people. Then she followed him outside They stood there for a while in the dark, which was broken by the clear moonlight, staring at each other for a long moment. Harper almost took a step forward, but sanity grabbed her just in time. This was serious business. And though she hadn't been in a relationship in what seemed forever, this was no time to play games, even if Gabe Walker made every female part of her body stand up and beg.

"Well." She walked up onto the porch. "See you in the morning. I'll leave the side door unlocked in case you need anything."

"I won't, but thanks." He paused. "If you're up at six thirty, I make a mean cup of coffee."

"And I've got sweet rolls," she told him. "See you then."

She let herself into the little building before she did something stupid and embarrassed herself. Tomorrow, she would ask Stone Jacobs everything about this man in the hopes he had some secret quirk that would help her shut down her hormones. But, for tonight, she might have to resort to the vibrator that had been her companion for such a long time.

CHAPTER 3

Harper wriggled her body beneath the press of male muscle, feeling the hard planes of his chest, his abs, his lower body. The thick length of his cock pushed against her thigh, and she wanted to tell him, "Not there. Inside me."

The first time he'd slid his hard length into her, she wasn't sure she could take it all. Abstinence had made the inner muscles of her sex tighten and become less flexible. Her vibrator was a very poor substitute for the real thing. She'd never been one for using it much, but she hadn't been with a man for so long it was her only resources when she got desperate. On the other hand, the anticipation of Gabe's rigid thick length stretching those muscles sent heat waves through her body and made her nipples harden to painful peaks.

Gabe cruised his lips, unexpectedly soft, over

the line of her jaw and down her neck, waking up all the little nerves clustered there. His mouth was a combination of firm and soft, teasing and tantalizing. Every place he touched her, nerves sparked and sent slivers of sexual hunger to her core.

Now he moved down her body, stroking her skin with hands that were hard but at the same time gentle. He traced the outline of her breasts, pausing at each to tweak each nipple and give it a light tug. Then he coasted those same fingers over the curve of her stomach, using the tips to outline the crease where hip and thigh met.

Sliding slowly down her body, he nudged her thighs apart with his shoulders, the breadth of them pushing her legs far apart and exposing every inch of her sex to him. The pulse that had begun to throb in those inner muscles intensified, and she couldn't help the little cries of pleasure that drifted from her mouth.

"That's it," he urged in his deep voice, the one that made her pulse race. "Let yourself go, Harper. Give me all you've got."

Yes, that was what she wanted. When he slid two fingers into her wet heat, she clamped down on them and pushed against the feeling. She matched the movement of her hips with the stroking of his fingers, letting out another moan when he added a third finger.

Oh god!

She wanted to come, but more than that, she wanted him inside her when she did, his hard cock filling her.

The touch of his tongue on her swollen clit sent electric shockwaves through her, and she dug her heels into the bed to push herself more tightly to his mouth. God, this was like nothing else she'd ever experienced, sexual pleasure that drove her out of her mind.

"Inside," she urged. "Now."

His low laugh vibrated against her, and the muscles of her sex clenched and throbbed.

She cried out in protest when he slid his fingers out, but then she heard the rip of foil and the snap of elastic, and then he was there. Inside her. That magnificent cock filling every inch of her.

Gabe pushed her knees back, widening her even more as his thick shaft stretched her inner walls.

"Go with it, darlin'," he urged. "Let go. Come on. Let go. Now."

And she did, letting the intensity of the sensations roll over her. He drove into her again and again, that magnificent shaft stretching her and rubbing all her nerves. More and more and more, until, at last, he slid his hands beneath the cheeks of her ass, lifting her more tightly to him, as they both exploded in body-clenching spasms.

When the last one had faded, she let her legs fall apart and reached down to close her fingers around his cock. She opened her eyes and smiled at…

Nothing?

What the hell?

She glanced around.

Good god. She was lying in her bed, her nightgown rucked up to her waist, working her vibrator to death as the orgasm faded. What the fuck? She didn't even remember taking the toy from her nightstand drawer, slathering lubricant on it, and sliding it into her body. Was she losing her mind?

She froze, easing the toy from her body and tossing it to the side. She hadn't used it in forever. Hadn't *wanted* to use it. Hadn't had even a passing interest in sex. All she ever focused on was her wolves.

She lay there for a long moment, catching her breath, her body still weak from the intensity of the orgasm. Now she wondered if she'd made any noise. Could Gabe Walker have heard her if she did? What on earth would he think? She was glad her bedroom was on the opposite side of the house from his tent, so there wasn't a chance he could see her, since she'd left the curtains open.

Good lord.

It had to be the Texas drawl. She wasn't given to being affected by things like that, but holy shit. Who could resist it? Deep. Slow. Sexy.

She pulled the covers over her heated face,

trying to hide in the darkness. At least she hadn't had any nightmares or slept uneasily.

Good lord, Harper. Get your shit together.

She lay there for a few minutes, her body sweaty and little aftershocks still pulsing through her. A shower. That was what she needed. A very cold one. And then a pot of coffee so she could get her shit together before she had to face Gabe Walker.

What time was it?

She glanced at her little clock. Four a.m. Great. Well, she'd get her day started extra early, that was for sure. A cold shower and hot coffee. Alrighty.

On her way to the kitchen, she peeked out the back window and saw a lantern glowing at the entrance to the tent. Holy shit. Didn't the man ever sleep? Please god, she hadn't made any noise in her sexual frenzy that carried outside.

Well, she would put the coffee on and, when it was ready, offer him some, if he hadn't brewed his own by then.

And figure out how she was going to face him.

GABE WAS SO USED to sleeping in small snaches that he was always up before anyone else, long before the sun rose. He was startled when a light went on in the office building. Did Harper suffer from the same kind of insomnia he did? What did she do when she woke up this early? At what hour did she begin checking on her wolves?

Her shadow moved againt the curtains, and he wondered if she wore a nightgown or pajamas? Or slept in the nude.

What the hell?

What was the matter with him? He was here in the role of protector, not some horny, scruffy guy whose dick sent him messages. She was off limits. It pissed him off that the first time he had a strong urge for a woman, it had to be one who had "untouchable" written all over her. Stone Jacobs would strip his hide if he got handsy with a client, and rightfully so.

But damn! She was the sexiest woman he'd seen in what seemed forever. Maybe it was her natural beauty, unadorned by any makeup. She obviously didn't need any out here, but he got the feeling it wasn't a priority for her anyway. And the jeans and T-shirt that molded to her body only enhanced her lithe, toned figure. A figure he wanted to run his hands over her sexy curves.

Not to mention the fact that she was smart as a whip. He hadn't had much luck in finding women with brains, but that was proably because he never got above their neck. Harper was unique. Too bad this was a job because…

Because nothing, idiot. Zip up your dick and stick to

business. Besides, she hasn't shown the least bit of interest in the fact that you're a male. Well, hell, Walker. Get your act together before you get your ass handed to you. By Harper and Stone both.

He checked to see if the coffee pot he'd set to brewing on the campfire was done yet. Almost. A good shot of caffeine was what he needed to straighten out his brain. Almost finished.

He stretched then stood looking out over the acres of land rolling away from him, broken by clusters of trees and piles of rocks that couldn't quite be called mountains, not even mini ones, but still created a place for the animals to climb. The moonlight had not quite faded yet, and his eye was caught by a wolf perched atop a tall, rocky pile. No matter what, they were magnificent animals.

He knew that Yellowstone was the flagship of the National Park Service and a favorite to millions of visitors each year. It had the distinction of being the world's frst national park and covered more than two million acres. Many other species of wildlife inhabited the place that were not predators, , balancing out the population. Some entrances to Wolf World were open for limited amounts of time, and one was open all year round.

Harper gave tours to visitors on a scheduled basis, and he wondered how she kept them safe from the wolves. There were campgrounds with reservations booked way in advance. Lodges were scattered over the acreage as well as campgrounds for people like Gabe who preferred a natural setup. Stone Jacobs' father owned a lodge about a half hour from the wolf preserve, and Gabe planned to visit him this morning and get as many details about the park and the ranchers as possible.

The man had spent ten years in the Marine Corps before retiring and deciding to open the lodge. Now he had rooms blocked off for his team until they found more permanent lodgings.

He knew the other members of the team would be staying there until they got their assignments. He also knew Stone wanted a place for the entire group to live in close proximity to him and felt West Yellowstone would work for their situation as a team.

When the coffee was ready, he was about to pour some in his stone mug when the back door to the office opened and Harper poked her head out.

"I've got my special brew ready in here," she told him, "if you want a change from campfire coffee."

He stared at her for a moment, the waning moon casting light on her freshly scrubbed skin and the silky strands of her blonde hair pulled back in a long ponytail. A T-shirt with *Wolf Preserve* on it and a sketch of a wolf molded to her breasts, and worn jeans clung to her hips. He'd better take himself in hand—in more ways than one—if he was going to be spending a lot of time with her. Sex hadn't been more than a habit or exercise with him for so long that the underlying feelings wriggling to the surface were unfamiliar. And dangerous.

Business, asshole, he told himself.

But he couldn't recall the last time his body had reacted so instantly to a woman. Swallowing a curse and sending a message to himself, he dumped his coffee and carried his empty mug to the doorway.

"I think yours sounds a lot tastier," he told her and followed her into the kitchen.

He was right. It had a rich flavor without being bitter and woke up his brain, which he desperately needed.

"You'll like connecting with John Jacobs," Harper told him. "He's solid. And he's as much into the wolves as I am."

Gabe had done some reading on gray wolves when he got this assignment. He knew gray had nothing to do with their color but meant they were timber wolves. Their color ranged from solid white or brown to black, and they looked somewhat like German shepherds. The one they'd seen last night had been a solid black. They lived in packs, and he'd have to remember to ask Harper how she handled that, especially when treating a sick animal or collaring them with a homing signal. He'd pick John Jacobs' brain, too.

"Good coffee." He raised his mug to her.

"One of my few luxuries." She grinned. "I order it from a place that makes special blends."

"Smart." He nodded. "I imagine it can get pretty lonely out here with only a couple of college kids, a pack of wolves, and no specialty groceries. Not to mention adult companionship."

She laughed, a musical sound that made his treacherous cock tingle.

"Not as busy as I am. Tracking the wolves, making sure they're healthy, giving tours, and fighting with Montana about regulations."

"The state doesn't like the wolves?"

She shrugged. "Depends who's in office. And who's exerting political pressure. Right now, the ranchers are flexing their muscles and looking to use any means to get rid of me. That's why we're in the situation we are."

Gabe drained his mug.

"You think it's too early to hit up John Jacobs?"

"No, he's got guests who are early risers. And I imagine your team that's there are also."

"Then I'll be on my way."

He had to battle an unwanted urge to pull her close to him and taste her lips but managed instead to rinse his mug and set it by the sink.

"See you later," she told him. "I fix lunch around one o'clock if you're interested."

"I'll take you up on it. Give me a chance to do

some exploring between now and then. See you later."

And he got the hell out of there before he did or said anything to embarrass himself.

THE LODGE WAS busy with very early morning activity when Gabe arrived. He made his way through the lobby with the big cathedral ceiling to the dining room already filled with guests. It didn't take him long to locate the table where the rest of his team were eating breakfast.

He noticed that Pierce, relaxed yet alert, sat beside Edge's chair. Apparently, the lodge had no restrictions on animals, or maybe John Jacobs had made an exception for the Brotherhood Protectors.

"Looks like we're all up with the birds today." Justice Kane grinned.

"Nothing new about that," Ridge Ridgely said. "I think we're all used to early hours and little sleep after Afghanistan. Gabe, the grub's real good here. Better fill up a plate before it's all gone."

Gabe did just that and managed a couple forkfuls of food before the questions started.

"See the wolves yet?" Justice asked.

"Last night, Harper Young gave me a tour of the preserve. Magnificent animals, I gotta say."

"What's she like?"

Sexy in a hot, natural way.

Shut the fuck up.

"Very nice, very well informed about what she's doing, and totally dedicated to her wolves." He took a sip of coffee. "And last night we got shot at."

Well, at least scoped out.

They all stared at him.

"Give," Justice said.

Gabe told him about the ranch hand watching them from the trees, rifle across his thighs.

"Harper said he works for Ed Culhane, who is apparently one of the top ranchers around here, money and property wise. I'd lay odds he's the one who took a shot at her. I want to dig around and find out all I can about him."

"We can help," Wade Fielding told him. "None of us are on assignment yet. We can be tourists sightseeing in the area and hanging out at some local spots."

"Good idea," Ridge agreed. "Tourists ask a lot of questions. Right?"

Wade laughed. "Sometimes too many. Right?"

"No shit." Gabe nodded his head.

"So, you need backup?" Justice asked.

"Not yet." Gabe shook his head. "They're still playing games. I hope to cut those off before they get more serious, but I'll keep Stone in the loop, of course."

They had just finished eating when John Jacobs made his way to their table and pulled out a chair.

"Nature and animal lovers do have healthy appetites," he joked. "We've not met yet, but I understand you work on my son's team. He assigned you to the wolf preserve, right? Happy to meet you." He shook Gabe's hand. "John Jacobs."

"Gabe Walker." Gabe nodded. "A pleasure to meet you."

"We're glad to have you guys here," John told them. "Politics can make a mess of things, and it's vital to remember the importance of the wolf. Montana's one of a handful of states that still has a wolf preserve, and a lot of people would like to see it gone. Want to bring back open hunting. Puts Harper Young and her group in a dangerous position."

"No kidding." Gabe nodded. "I'd like to find out a lot more about Ed Culhane and his friends."

"First of all, he's the richest rancher around here." John took a sip of his coffee. "The Four Diamond Ranch is ten thousand acres plus and runs four thousand head of cattle at any one time."

"Big operation," Gabe commented.

"No shit. And it's got longevity. Ed's the fourth generation to run the ranch, and he keeps increasing the size of the herd. He's got a shitpile of money and throws it around where he needs to."

"What's his beef with the wolves? They're all in the preserve enclosure."

"It's twofold," John answered. "One, he says they get out of the fencing and attack his cattle, although no one has ever seen evidence of it. And two, he's a hunter. Hunting season's been expanded recently, but he wants open season for himself and his friends."

"And he carries the weight," Ridge mused.

"He does. And he funds a lot of political campaigns, including the sheriff's." John studied his empty cup for a moment. "You didn't hear me say this, but I've heard he's talked about 'eliminating' people who oppose him."

"Well, shit." Gabe leaned forward. "Can you get me a complete history on this guy so I can study it?"

"Yes, I can. Just be careful where you poke the bear. I'm telling you, this guy would have no qualms about making you disappear." Then he smiled. "Of course, he has no idea who he's dealing with here."

The men chuckled.

"Amen to that," Wade told him.

"I'll check into his friend, Frank Winslow, for you, too," John told them. "Those guys are joined at the hip, although Ed has more power and uses it even on his friends."

"I thought I might hang out in town for a bit,"

Gabe told him. "Kind of get a feel for the atmosphere."

"Just remember they'll be sizing you up, too," John told him. "Maybe a couple of the others here should scope things out. I think it's best to keep you in the background. At least for now."

"Maybe you're right," Gabe agreed. "In that case, I might drive around the park and get a feel for everything. Whoever goes into town, shoot me whatever you manage to dig up. I want to see if Harper's got any tours booked. We didn't get into that, and I want to be prepared."

"Good idea." John nodded. "Well, I'm around here for anything you need. I told Stone I want to help as much as I can."

"We appreciate it," Justice told him. "And we like having a purpose now that the military's behind us. Win, win."

"Gabe, text me your phone number. When I get some info, I'll shoot it to you."

"Thanks. I texted Stone this morning and asked him to have Hank's computer guru, Swede, dig into the two of them, also." He pushed back from the table. "I guess I'll get going. "Where do I pay for breakfast?"

"No place." John shook his head. "I told Stone the rooms are on the house but the meals are on you guys. I'm part of this, too."

"Thank you." Gabe nodded at the others. "Let's

check in around noon and see what the morning brought. Justice, you want to be point man?"

"Works for me."

"Okay, then."

RESTLESS, trying to absorb the information, Ed paced his den. This was a new wrinkle, and it irritated him, made him uneasy.

"Okay. First let's find out a little more about the men you saw this morning," he began." I do have something else I want you to find a way to check out, though. Four men who look a little out of place compared to his other customers checked into the lodge Jacobs owns. I think they might be former military, like him. In any event, I want to know what they're doing here and why."

"I think you are getting overly sensitive. We get all kinds of visitors here. Most of them are nature or animal lovers of one kind or another. They come here to take the tours. I don't want them getting in our way."

"I'm hosting the Cattlemen's Association at Four Diamond next week," Ed told him. "I can see if they've picked up any gossip, too."

"Just keep it on the downlow, like you said. If they are here to stick their nose in our business, we need to know it and stop it. And without shooting anyone. Let's see if we can get this under control. Meanwhile, go do your usual snooping and see what you can find out. But don't draw attention to yourself. We don't need that. Just be a genial rancher welcoming folks to this area."

Gabe had just finished his last cup of coffee and was getting ready to leave when a man walked into the dining room who lit up all his spidey senses. He immediately did not like him. The man looked like a regular rancher, just shaking hands with visitors to the area and greeting people he knew. Stone had told him longtime residents often did that. Called it Yellowstone hospitality.

But Gabe smelled rich rancher across the room. Powerful. Arrogant. Which of the men Harper mentioned was this? Was it his ranch hand who had taken shots at Harper?

Gabe was suspicious of everyone he didn't know—and some people he did—and he didn't see why the hell a rancher with thousands of acres to manage would be hanging out with tourists. They didn't put dollars in his pocket, and he said so to the others.

"Maybe he just likes talking to people," Ridge mused. "On the other hand, I'm with you. I'm suspicious of everyone. It's how we've survived for so long."

"And maybe he's just nosy," Gabe added, "but I get a bad vibe from him.

"Well, Stone doesn't want us kicking any tin cans down the highway unless we have proof of something," Ridge reminded him. "And I don't want to cause a scene at his dad's place. I think taking this little trip into West Yellowstone and scoping out the situation will make a difference. We've learned what to look for."

"And what? Ask if anyone's been shooting at Harper Young? Or shown an unnatural interest in John Jacobs' guests?" He snorted. "That's really keeping it on the downlow."

"No worries. I'd know if they did without asking. And I can tell you who our visitor is."

Gabe and Ridge had been so engrossed in their conversation they hadn't heard John approach the table until he pulled out a chair and sat down.

"We'd better brush up on our skills," Ridge commented. "We never let people sneak up on us."

"And you won't now," John assured them. "The guy who came in is Frank Winslow. More money than brains and Ed Culhane's sidekick He owns a ranch nearly as large as Culhane's and does whatever Ed tells him to, but don't think that makes him stupid. The two of them have controlled this area for a long time."

"We'll keep that in mind," Ridge told him.

"He has the ranch next to the wolf preserve," John told them. "It was one of Culhane's hands who took a shot at us last night. I don't consider them very friendly, but they do wield a lot of power. Especially Culhane, so it's good to keep an eye on them."

"Oh, we will," Gabe promised him "Count on it."

"I think if you just scope out the town," John continued, "and do stuff like visit the sporting goods store, the hunting store, like that, you'll be good. Stop in for a cup of coffee. People will ask you questions, and those questions might give you a clue if something is in the wind."

"Good idea." Justice nodded. "If we could blend in at the sandbox, we can sure do it here."

"What you're angling for'" John went on, "is a hint that there's a campaign against the wolf preserve being discussed. Buy some touristy stuff then come back here and we'll chew on it."

"Sounds good." Ridge nodded. "Okay, guys, let's hit the road. Dig up anything we can that will help Gabe."

CHAPTER 4

FRANK FROWNED INTO HIS MUG. "I checked out the guests at John Jacobs' lodge."

He and Ed were sitting in Ed's den with their morning coffee, reviewing the situation. He had made a stop at the lodge as Ed had suggested and come here to report. Neither of them was happy with the fact they hadn't been able to find out a single thing about the man who'd shown up at Yellowstone Wolf Preserve out of no place. How could someone be so invisible? More than that, how could someone with Ed's connections not find a single fact from anyone?

"Why?"

"I bet my prize steer he's connected in some way to Stone Jacobs, John's son," Frank mused. "In fact, they look like they're part of some kind of paramilitary organization that plans on saving the world."

Ed burst out laughing. "Are you for real? Stone's just a used-up military grunge who left the Army because he couldn't take it anymore. We get them all the time, remember?"

Frank shook his head. "I think it's different this time. He's John Jacobs' son, and that man doesn't stand for any bullshit."

"He doesn't stand for anything," Ed corrected. "He's just a washed-up Marine who spends his days running that lodge and running tours. People make shit up because it sounds good and they like to glamorize people."

"You know the Young woman is hounding the state and all the government organizations to shorten the hunting season again and change the rules about wolves. She's on a crusade."

"She's a damn pain in the ass, is what she is," Ed told him. "Life would be so much easier if we could just scare her the hell away."

"Easy isn't always available," Frank pointed out. "And I don't think a stray shot now and then is going to scare her off."

"We can't get rid of her," Ed pointed out. "At least not right away or in a way that makes people ask questions. I still think if we do this right, we can scare the shit out of her, and she'll decide it isn't worth her effort to stay here and fight us.""

"Then we'd better come up with something more than a stray shot now and then. She's got a guy there since last night who's part of the group at the lodge. I saw him with them this morning. We don't want all-out war, Ed. That could bring us bigger trouble than we've already got.

"No, but we need some leverage. And I still think if we can scare the shit out of the Young woman, we'll accomplish what we want. Make her decide to finally pack up and leave."

"I hope you're right because we've got a hunting party coming for their visit in two weeks, and we don't need her making their lives miserable."

"She can't do anything if they follow the rules," Frank reminded him.

"She can hassle them, like she's done before. And having one of those guys around her at all times will make that a lot easier."

"Let me find out more about them, and we can reassess the situation. But I'm telling you, Ed, we have to get rid of her."

"And we will. We just need to know what we're up against so we can plan. I don't think it'll just be one guy involved with her. I know you couldn't ask John about the guys at the lodge…"

"Not at the moment. I was going to manage an introduction, but they left before I could do it without being obvious."

"We'll figure it out. Meanwhile, West Yellowstone is not that big. Maybe they went into town. See if you can run into them or get some gossip from the store owners. Give me a call and let me know how it goes."

"Will do. We'll get rid of that bitch one way or another."

"But with smarts, Frank. With smarts."

"Meanwhile, I'll have one of my guys keep an eye on the woman and the man at all times. I don't want to be caught off guard."

HARPER HAD JUST BACKED the ATV out of the lean-to when Gabe drove up and parked his truck.

"Taking a ride again?" he asked.

"Just some chores. I have a malfunctioning collar that I need to check on. Make sure it's still on the wolf. And I want to get some photos for a new brochure I'm putting together."

"Yeah, Stone said you give tours of the preserve. Is that what these are for? Tourist stuff?"

She nodded. "Partially. I also use them to lobby government organizations and for funds that raise money to protect wolves. You should come along for the ride."

"I should. Especially if I'm here to protect you. I don't want you riding the preserve without me."

She studied his face. "You really think these guys would try to kill me?"

"No," he told her in that Texas drawl, "but they'll do everything they can to scare you off."

"Then they need a bigger bag of tricks. But come on. I will feel better with you along."

Although maybe that's not such a god thing, she told herself. Remnants of her dream still clung to her brain.

After swallowing a sigh, she lifted the equipment bag she'd placed next to her on the seat and tucked it on the floor. But first, she pulled out a small gadget that she turned on and held up in front of her.

"GPS locator," she told Gabe. "It's how I find the wolves when I want to or need to. They each have their own code, so I know what's what." She fiddled with the dials before setting the gadget in a cupholder. Then she backed around and took off.

As they drove, she periodically stopped, held up the locator, and marked numbers off on a tablet she also had with her.

"Here, I can do that." Gabe took the locator from her. "You've got enough to do with driving."

"Okay, if you're sure that—"

"You aren't going to ask a veteran of Middle East battles if he knows how to use this. Right?"

Heat flushed her cheeks. "No. Of course not."

Stupid.

It worked more efficiently with the two of them. She usually tried to take one of her part-time assistants with her, but today she'd been itchy doing nothing but sitting around and needed to be out doing something. Besides, a faulty collar could mean too many bad things. Including a dead wolf.

They had already identified and checked off several wolves on her sheet before they finally found the one she was looking for. That collar itself had caught on the gnarly limb of a juniper bush, and the wolf thrashed about trying to get loose. Gabe watched her as she lifted a syringe gun from her bag and got close enough to the wolf to inject him. When he was finally quiet, they climbed out of the ATV, and Harper showed Gabe what to do while she freed and reprogrammed the collar.

"I have to say I admire you," he said as they drove off. "I don't think I know another woman who would play patty cake with a wolf."

Harper laughed. "Me, either. And it takes a lot of training to do it just right without endangering the wolf or yourself. Jim Haggerty was a great teacher. I worked for him here for three years before he retired and I got hired into his job."

"They made a smart move," Gabe told her. "I'd say you're doing a damn fine job."

Harper was more used to criticism than compliments, so when heat crept up her face, she bent down to fiddle in the bag while she got her hormones under control again. A breeze drifted across her face, carrying with it a trace of Gabe's outdoorsy cologne. At once, remnants of her dream flashed in her brain, and her face got even hotter. She lifted the bag and shifted on the seat so she could face away from the hot guy next to her.

"You okay?" he asked.

"Yes, fine." *Not.* "I'm checking for another locator. Ah, here we go."

She pulled it out, praying he wouldn't ask her what was wrong with the other one since her answer would be *nothing.*

"All set?"

"Yes. Yes, fine." *Not.*

"Why don't I drive?" he suggested. "That way you can focus all your attention on locating the wolves."

And why hadn't she thought of that before? Because her brain was still addled by an erotic dream.

They switched places, and Harper settled herself with her equipment.

They had reached a far corner of the preserve when Gabe touched her leg.

"Unfriendlies at nine o'clock," he told her in a low voice.

She glanced to her left, and sure enough, tonight there were two, not one, ranch hands sitting on their horses, silently watching. One of them had a rifle lying across his thighs, but she wasn't worried he might use it. Not so close to last night's episode. Their goal was to frighten her, not kill her.

Yet.

"Maybe we should cut this little trip short," Gabe suggested.

Harper shook her head. "If they wanted to shoot, they would. Like the guy last night. They're only trying to frighten me, but instead they are making me mad. Let's keep moving."

Gabe nodded. "Okay."

But she noticed that he lifted the rifle he had placed between them and made sure the men could see it before he set it down again.

"Two can play that game," Gabe told her. "Okay, all set? Here we go."

It took nearly an hour before Harper had all the wolves recorded. The two ranch hands had followed along the one fence line until they turned away from that area.

"They won't follow us anymore," Harper said. "They think what they did is enough to scare the shit out of me. They won't shoot except at night when they think I won't see them. They wait until I do my late tours. We're good."

Still, she noticed that Gabe had placed the rifle in such a way he could grab it and shoot in a fraction of seconds.

About fifteen minutes later, almost by accident, they found another wolf with the wonky collar that was just starting to fail. She felt Gabe watching her, fascinated, as they got close enough for Harper to shoot her tranquilizer dart into the animal.

"Now we just have to wait for the drug to take effect, which only takes a few seconds."

He was right at her side when at last she climbed out and moved to the unconscious animal.

"You sure this is safe?" he asked.

"I've been doing this a long time," she assured him. "Trust me. We're good."

She sensed him next to her as she knelt beside the tranquilized wolf and changed out his collar. The animal just lay there, eyes closed, breathing slowly.

"We'll keep checking, in case there's another one down and the signal isn't working," she told Gabe.

"Every once in a while, one of these malfunctions. I just needed to make sure someone hadn't aimed over the fence and shot one of the wolves. Or somehow stolen the collar." She stood up and gathered her equipment. "We're good. Let's finish the tour. Not too many more to check, and we should do all of them while we're out here.."

By the time they were finished, it was dark.

"You must be hungry," Harper told Gabe as she had him turn back to the office. "Sorry. I tend to get lost in what I'm doing."

"I'm good, although I'll never turn down food."

"I can make some sandwiches when we get back. One of my students should be here by then, and we'll be working on bringing the records up to date. Pretty boring work, just so you know."

"After staring down the sandbox for hours at a time," he told her, "nothing bores me. I'll happily take a sandwich, but then I think I want to take another tour of the preserve while you're working. I want to take some pictures so the guys have a visual of the place. Also, if any of your stalkers are out there again, I want to get pictures of them. Maybe show them this isn't one-sided."

"Have at it," she told him. "Any message like that we can send is better for me."

CORY EVERHART, one of the students, was waiting at the office when they got back. Harper introduced Gabe to him, fixed lunch for all of them, then she and Cory went to work on a project in the office. Harper had plugged the ATV in when they'd gotten back, and when he checked, he found it close to fully charged, so he headed out into the preserve.

The environment really was gorgeous, especially with the late-summer colors. Harper had told him that temps in those months hovered in the low seventies, which made her daily rides comfortable. Sometimes in early fall it could get as hot as eighty-five, which was a Yellowstone version of Indian summer, but it was pretty comfortable otherwise.

Forests covered roughly 80 percent of the park, but there were plenty of open spaces in the preserve where the animals could roam. Stone hadn't given him a lot of info, saying Harper would fill him in. He did, however, warn him the bison rut began on August 3, which made hunting by the wolves easy for them, but could be dangerous to visitors if not careful. Better to be extra careful during that season because there were plenty of bison for the wolves to feed on.

He drove slowly, not just along the perimeter but crisscrossing the rest of it to familiarize himself with the landscape: the trees and piles of rocks and hills. He spotted a number of wolves on his journey, but, as Harper had said, if he didn't bother them, they didn't bother him. The ones he spotted standing on a hill or an outcropping looked like majestic animals staking their claim on the land. He'd been a hunter as a teenager, but he couldn't for the life of him see why anyone would want to kill these magnificent animals just for sport, especially with the dwindling population.

He also made a mental note of places just outside the perimeter where Harper's stalkers could watch her and decided to take pictures of some of them to share with Stone. He was leaning back in his seat,studying a cluster of lodgepole pines when he spotted what had to be one of the ranch hands, slouched in his saddle like the man earlier. Didn't these people have anything else to do? What about the ranch that obviously required a lot of people to run it? Could Ed Culhane spare a hand or two just to torment Harper?

Gabe thought about just driving off, but instead, he took his phone from his pocket again and snapped a few pictures of the man. He wanted the word to be passed that just like Culhane had his men watching Harper, she had her own team now keeping an eye on them. Then he just sat, staring at him, until the man nudged his horse with his heels and moved off at a slow trot.

He knew plenty about power-hungry men and how they went after people who pissed them off or interfered with their lives. He needed to talk to Stone so they could put a plan together. He punched the man's number into his phone.

"What's going on?" Stone asked.

"Culhane's sent someone to spy on Harper again. I'm sending you a couple of pictures of him, but my guess is he's just a ranch hand carrying out orders. Here they come."

"I know this guy," Stone told him when he'd seen the photos. He's one of Culhane's top hands. Been with him a long time. Rumor had it he was the one who set fire to the barn at a neighboring ranch, trying to chase the guy away. Culhane had been trying to buy his land."

"What an asshole."

"And dangerous," Stone warned.

"More than the others?"

"He's been with Culhane longer than anyone else and is also a crack shot with a rifle. Even wins competitions."

Gabe snorted. "How do you think he'd do against a SEAL sniper?"

"Not well, unless he hid well and got off the first shot. I'm thinking I might send some backup who can cover the hours at night when you need to sleep, few as they might be."

A laugh rumbled out of his throat. "Sleep? You mean we're actually allowed to do that?"

"Yeah, yeah, yeah. Smartass. I'll send one of the guys along after dinner. I thought of trying to sneak him in, but actually it's better if Culhane knows we're doubling up. Might make him think twice about what he does."

"Good idea," Gabe agreed. "I'll tell Harper. I'm sure she won't fight us on this. If she's dead, she can't play with her wolves."

"Yeah, she's smart all right."

"You guys getting along okay?" Stone asked.

"No problems," Gabe assured him. "She's smart, Stone, and certainly knows her wolves. I think it sucks that she doesn't get the support from the government organizations she needs and that the little clan of powerful ranchers think they can run over her. She doesn't deserve to have men on horseback stalking her or the sheriff's department telling her they can't do anything for her until something happens. I guess they didn't consider being shot at in that category."

"I've had the other guys doing their best to act like tourists. I sent them into West Yellowstone, as you know, to see what they can dig up."

"You don't think Culhane will figure out what's going on and get pissed?"

Stone barked a laugh. "I hope he does. With this group being permanently headquartered here, he might think twice about being an asshole. But I want to get as much feedback on him as I can. And on Frank Winslow. They're the two lead jackasses. If they know we'll be permanently keeping an eye on them, they might back off. In any event, if there's another shot fired, I'll pay a little call. Keep taking those pictures. I'll let you know who your backup is going to be."

"Thanks, Stone. I'll be in touch."

He disconnected and put the ATV in gear again. His plan was to be as visible as possible. The idiots might not think twice about shooting at Harper, but he hoped they'd take a breath before using him for target practice. It was close to six by the time he figured he'd made himself visible enough. The ranch hand he'd spotted showed again up after about two hours, but he seemed to be focused on checking Gabe out more than anything else. He showed up twice more, took a good look, then headed away from the preserve. Gabe took pictures of him both times and made it obvious that was what he was doing.

Gabe also familiarized himself with more areas of the property and its landscape. Just like overseas in the sandbox, the more he imprinted the landscape on his mind, the better he was able to deal with the enemy. He also enjoyed watching the wolves, who kept their distance but seemed as interested in him as he was in them.

Stone called as he was about to quit for the day.

"Dig up any dirt?" Gabe asked.

"Working on it. We learned the Ed Culhane is the model for the biggest asshole in the world. That he has enough money to buy and sell West Yellowstone twice, and he's sworn to get rid of Harper and the wolves one way or another. And to do it so it doesn't come back on him."

"Figured as much," Gabe agreed.

"But he's also said if he has to make a choice, he'll rid the place of Harper. Believes if he does, the organizations won't want to send anyone else in. He may be right. And he's got everyone in the town and the county so far under this thumb they aren't about to give him any garbage about it."

"We can't let that happen."

"And we won't. I promise you that. I'm sending Ridge later for the night shift. He'll check in with you when he gets there. Keep a sharp eye out for everything."

"As always." He disconnected the call.

The student helper was just pulling out of the parking area when he drove up to the office. Harper was standing on the porch, waving good-bye, and she turned and grinned at him.

"You must have really enjoyed yourself out there to be gone for so long."

"It's impressive out there, but I also spotted your spy from Culhane's ranch twice. I took some pictures so he knows we are also keeping an eye on him."

He'd also taken his time out there so he wouldn't have a hard-on poking at his fly when he got back. It had been a long time since a woman affected him this way. When he first arrived at the office, he thought his reaction was just to a beautiful woman with natural beauty. But as the hours passed and he spent one-on-one time with her, he'd realized he might have a problem. He hadn't been with a woman in a while, which left him two choices: ask Stone to suggest a place he could pick one up for a night, which didn't appeal to him even a little, or else give his good right hand some exercise. He'd better be sure to zip his tent securely tonight just in case, for whatever reason, Harper came looking for him.

"That's a good idea. Stone called to tell me he had the rest of you playing tourist in town to see what they could hear. Small towns are always full of gossips, and their people love to dish it up."

"Normally, we'd keep a low profile when we arrive somewhere," he explained to her, "but in this situation, it's a little different. We want Culhane to know reinforcements have arrived and he should back off and adjust his plans. Hopefully, it will send him to the organizations that have reduced the regulations for hunting, and they'll reinstate some of them. And maybe pay for a permanent guard for Yellowstone Wolf Preserve."

"God. That would be so wonderful."

She pulled the ponytail holder from her hair and ran her fingers through the streaky-blonde tresses. Gabe's fingers itched to be the ones doing that. If he didn't get his libido under control, Stone would pull him from this assignment, and that would be a disaster. Maybe after they took care of these assholes he could ask Harper out on a real date. Of course, he hadn't been on one himself in so long, he wasn't sure he'd know how to act.

"I'm grilling again tonight," she told him. "Unless you're married to whatever you've got in your ice chest, I've got barbecued chicken and corn."

"Are you sure? I don't want to impose."

"I'm happy for the company. Give me forty-five minutes."

He wanted to give her the whole night and eat more than barbecue, but he just nodded and thanked her. Anything else would probably get him thrown out on his ass.

Still…

Maybe he had enough time to hide in his tent and relieve the pressure in his dick. Except, what if she came looking for him?

You are fucked, my man, and not in the right way. Get your act together.

CHAPTER 5

"THE NEWCOMERS AT JACOBS' lodge sure were asking a lot of questions." Frank flipped his beer bottle top in the waste basket. He wasn't in the mood for his usual bourbon, but he needed a drink after scoping out the activity in town today.

"About what?" Ed sipped his drink.

"Oh, who the big shots in the area are. The top ranchers. They acted like they might be scoping out the job market, but they also were asking how the ranchers and all got along with the wolf preserve. What the hunting regulations are."

"Did they look like hunters to you? We can call the licensing office and see if there have been any new requests for permits. Or even questions about them."

"Already did that as soon as I left the lodge," Frank told him, "and the answer is no. Of course, they could just be scoping out the area. But you said they looked like they knew John Jacobs, so I'm thinking they're scoping out us and not anything else."

"They've got to be connected to the guy who showed up at Yellowstone Wolf Preserve yesterday. Strangers who don't look like our usual tourists can't be strangers. Ned said the guy with Harper Young spotted him twice today and took pictures of him both times. And now these guys who all look like they came from the same mold show up? I don't like it."

"John Jacobs is a long-time Marine," Frank reminded him. "Maybe these guys are all Marines, too."

Ed shook his head. "Stone Jacobs, his son, was Army. I'd say that's where these guys came from. And all five may be from the same team."

"Maybe they'll go back to where they came from pretty soon," Frank mused. "I hope it's before we have that big cattle auction and hunting party in a couple of weeks. We don't need them prowling the area and scaring off our clients."

"And I don't want to have to do anything drastic." Ed took another swallow of his drink. "We've worked too hard to get control of things. We have to figure out how to get rid of that female. We can't let her screw it up now."

"But we have to be careful," Frank reminded

him. "Nothing can come back on us, no matter how much we think we have control of things."

"You leave that to me. I'll make sure we have a plan in place that doesn't trace to us."

"You gonna have Don Bracken still keeping an eye on her?"

Ed nodded. "Got to. Have to monitor what's going on. He told me this guy spent most of the afternoon just riding around the preserve, as if he was checking on the wolves. But damn, you know he was looking for spies, which is why he took Don's picture. I told him, no more shooting. Just monitor what's going on and when and for how long this guy keeps riding around."

"You want to use a couple of my guys so we can change faces?" Frank asked.

"Might not be a bad idea," Ed mused. "They can use my horses. Let's work out a schedule. Change things up."

"Okay. Let's get to it."

"DINNER WAS GREAT." Gabe wiped his fingers on his napkin. "At this rate, you might never get rid of me."

Harper stared at him. "That might not be so bad. You'd keep all the bogeymen away."

"The goal is to shut them down permanently,

even if they are the ones with a lot of power. Nobody is invincible."

"We need the government and licensing people to work with us on that, on the hunting regulations, and, so far, they seem to side with the assholes with the money."

"Well," Gabe drawled, "we plan to figure out a way to make it happen and make it stick. If that means I'm here for the long haul, well, Stone wants it done whatever it takes."

Harper stared at him, a sliver of heat shimmying from her breasts to her belly and down between her thighs. She squeezed them together, thankful they were sitting at the small kitchen table so Gabe could not see his effect on her. She couldn't remember the last time she'd had sex of any kind, or even been with a man who turned her on.

Oh, wait. Last night's dream popped into her head, and another wave of heat flashed through her, suffusing her face as she remembered how she'd woken up that morning. What had she been thinking? *Not* thinking, that was the problem. Her long suppressed hormones had exploded in a flash, and there she was, riding her spasms with a toy she hadn't used in months.

Was it dangerous for her to have Gabe Walker here for more than another five minutes? What if they ended up in bed together? Would it wreck the situation? Would Stone pull his man and send her someone else? How would he even know? And if—bizarre thought—she made an overture to Gabe, how would he react? Was that a flicker of heat she'd seen in his eyes before? God knew he was sex on a stick, and she could see—

Get your act together, woman. Someone wants to kill you, or at least run you off. Where is there time for sex in there?

"You okay?" Gabe's voice interrupted her erotic reverie.

"Um, yes, fine. Just wondering if you were up for some ice cream?"

"Ice cream, huh?" His grin told her he didn't believe a word she'd said. "Sure, I could go for some."

He helped her clear the table, and while she took care if the few dishes, he cleaned the grill. Then they carried their ice cream outside to the porch and sat side by side on the little bench she had out there.

"This is nice," he said at last.

"I love it out here, just when the sun is going down. I can catch the last rays and the final heat of the day. The preserve has so many open spaces, unlike the rest of the park, that I can even watch animals from the distance. It's really the most peace I get."

"I feel it, too." He leaned forward to place his empty dish on the tree stump she used as a little table, and when he sat back, he leaned one arm across the back of the bench.

For a moment, she thought about shaking it off or just adjusting herself so she wasn't so close to him. But the touch of his body sent shimmers of sensation through her. While she knew she was courting trouble—she had known this guy less than forty-eight hours—he had elicited reactions from her that she hadn't felt in far too long. Her entire life—all her emotions—had been focused on her wolves. Was this a real feeling or just an over-reaction?

His large hand with its long fingers rested on the edge of her shoulder. Taking a breath, she edged a little closer to him. His fingers tightened just a fraction.

Do I even know what I'm doing?

"So, your social life out here must be pretty isolated." Gabe's comment broke the silence.

"Social life?" She gave a little laugh. "It's me and the wolves."

"I can't believe the men in West Yellowstone haven't been beating a path to your door at least to work with you."

Another laugh.

"I'm not exactly a popular person here, except with the wildlife people. They don't like me cutting into their hunting regulations or drawing money they think could go to other purposes. Besides, there are plenty of women who show up here looking for hot cowboys. No, I'm kind of on the outskirts."

Silence sat between them for a long moment until Gabe broke it.

"If I wasn't on assignment here, you'd be at the top of my list."

Harper chewed her bottom lip for a moment.

"What if, just for a tiny little moment, we pretended you're not. Just for a second."

"And what if that tiny moment turned into a longer one?" he asked. "What if it changed things between us so you didn't want me around anymore?"

"Never gonna happen, not matter what." She blew out a breath. "I mean it, Gabe. No commitment here. No anything. Just two people enjoying the evening."

Was that really her being so forward?

He was silent for so long, she was sure he was figuring out how to walk away from this.

"Friends, no matter what?"

"Promise."

"Okay, then."

He cupped her head, turning it so she faced him, and brushed his lips against hers. Flames instantly shot through her body. She had expected those lips to be rough, but they were smooth and sexy, warm and tender. He brushed his mouth back and forth against hers, each sweep lighting another finger of heat in her body. She didn't even remember this kind of sensation with a kiss before. She had either been kissing the wrong men or had been out of circulation so long she'd forgotten what it was like.

No, she'd have remembered a kiss like this. Especially when he traced the seam of her lips with his tongue and sensations cascaded through her like an erotic waterfall.

When he cupped her cheeks, turning her face more toward him, she wrapped her fingers around his wrists to hold him in place. She really wanted this kiss to go on forever, even though she wanted much, much more.

He prodded her lips apart and eased his tongue inside, sweeping the lining of her mouth and setting off flickers of flame. Boldly, she swept her own tongue over his, setting off an erotic dance that she could have done forever, if she hadn't wanted more from him.

Gabe pulled the band holding her hair in a tail and ran his fingers through the cascading curls, sliding them so he could cup her head and hold it in place. His fingers were warm, igniting every nerve in her scalp and sending shimmers of heat through her body. Her nipples hardened, and she had to squeeze her thighs to try and control the throbbing in her sex. Except for last night, she hadn't felt this sensation or arousal since…well, forever.

The kiss went on for what seemed forever, but that was okay with Harper. She had no desire to send it.

Except…

She wanted more. Much more.

Was she crazy? Stone was going to kill her if he found out. But then, who was to tell him? Not her. Not Gabe. Not the wolves.

When he broke the kiss and stood up, a flicker of disappointment snaked through her. Was it over already, when it had hardly begun?

"I don't really want the wolves spying on us," he joked, but his voice was thick with passion. "What about you?"

"As long as we're not moving to the tent," she teased. "I like my comfort."

"Ditto."

He took her hand and led her inside, waited while she locked the door then followed her to her bedroom. She gave thanks she'd made the bed that morning and tidied the place up. Before she could figure out what came next, Gabe turned her to him, cupped her chin, and gave her a kiss that scorched her to the soles of her feet. She was no novice at this, but she didn't remember ever being on the receiving end of a kiss so powerful. She opened her mouth wide to receive his tongue then slicked hers over his again and again.

He pulled her tight against him, sliding his hands down her spine until he could cup her ass and press her to him. It was hard to miss the thick, hard length of his cock as it imprinted itself against her sex. She twitched her hips back and forth, creating a friction that made his cock swell even more and the inner walls of her sex flutter.

GABE EASED his hands up the outline of her rib cage until he could cup both firm breasts in his palms. He squeezed, lightly, and felt her nipples harden even more, pressing into the center of his hands. He trapped them between his fingers and gently squeezed and was rewarded with a sharp intake of breath from the woman whose body was plastered to his.

He took her mouth again, thrusting his tongue inside, savoring the taste of her and hungry to taste other parts of her body.

"I think we have too many clothes on," he murmured, forcing himself to take a step back.

Harper never said a word, but when she moved away it was to pull the covers back on the bed and shove the pillows toward the headboard. Then she lifted her T-shirt by the hem and pulled it over her head.

Gabe nearly swallowed his tongue. Perfect breasts nestled in lacy cups, the femininity of them surprising him. He'd expected something more utilitarian, but this woman was a constant surprise. The plump mounds swelled over the top edge of the bra, and beneath the thin fabric he could see the dark outline of her nipples as they pressed into it.

He wanted to grab them and squeeze, but he didn't want to stop the strip tease going on in front of him. He watched as she reached behind her to unhook her bra and tossed it to the side where it landed with the discarded T-shirt. Gabe nearly swallowed his tongue as he looked at the round, firm mounds capped with rosy-pink nipples, and it was all he could do not to just reach out and grab them.

Harper studied him, a questioning look in her eyes.

"Maybe you haven't done this a lot," she teased in a shaky voice, "but both of us have to take our clothes off.

"Sometimes I think I've done it too much," he told her, "but no woman's ever had this kind of impact on me. And my clothes are coming off, believe me. But not until you are completely naked. And I think I should help you."

She undid her zipper, but when she would have pulled both her jeans and panties down her legs, Gabe knelt in front of her. Brushing her hands aside, he eased both the jeans and panties down her legs, helped her out of her shoes, and discarded the last of her clothing. The sight in front of him stole his breath.

Curls as blonde as those on her head formed a cloak for the most tempting sex he had ever seen. He had to restrain himself from throwing her onto the bed and thrusting into her, but he was determined to take his time. Kneeling before her, he traced the curves with the tips of his fingers, running them lightly through silken curls. He skimmed the tips of his fingers over the curve of her mound and finally allowed himself to ease them between the full lips of her sex.

Jesus!

What the hell are you doing, Walker?

Something he hadn't really enjoyed for a very long time. He prayed he wasn't screwing anything up.

She was slick and wet, and his cock nearly exploded. He hadn't given much thought to how he'd proceed, but he needed a taste of her in the worst way. Opening her lips with his thumbs, he drew a line from top of her sex to her opening with the tip of his tongue. When she shuddered and dug her fingers into his shoulders, he did it again. He hoped to fuck he didn't come in his jeans before he got to the really good part. He was starting to feel like a horny teenager.

Again and again he traced that wet channel of her sex, each caress drawing a shuddering breath from her. Finally, he eased her back onto the bed, spread her legs wide, and, returning to his knees, thrust his tongue deep inside her. When her inner muscles clenched around his touch, he began an in-and-out movement with his tongue, scraping her slick walls, moving faster and faster until she lifted her hips to him and came with an explosion, her inner walls spasming again and again. Pinching his tongue and sending him into overdrive. It took everything he had to keep his dick under control.

He rested his head on her mound, hands sliding beneath the cheeks of her ass to support her as she lay on the edge of the bed and giving him a moment to catch his breath. Jesus! This woman was a treasure, better than any he'd ever been with. He'd better not do anything to fuck this up.

"Are you going to take your clothes off, or is just one of us going to be naked?" she asked in a voice edged with a little laugh.

"Oh, they're coming off right now. I just need a second."

Rising to his feet, he stripped as fast as he could, remembering to pull the strip of condoms he never left home without from his wallet. Then he rearranged her on the bed so he could crawl up between her legs and cup her face in his palms.

"You take my breath away," he told her. "That

hasn't happened in a long time."

She studied his face carefully. "What is this, Gabe? What are we doing?"

How to give her answers he didn't even have yet.

"Let's just say we're getting to know and enjoy each other and maybe finding something good in this mess we're in."

It took a long moment for her to answer, one in which Gabe held his breath.

"I can go with that," she said at last. "Just so you know, it's been a long time for me, so I might not meet your expectations."

"Not to worry." He brushed his mouth over hers. "I haven't been that active myself, and certainly not with someone who stirs feelings in me the way you have. Let's just see where this goes. Meanwhile…"

Yes, meanwhile.

He kissed his way down her body, trailing his lips down her neck and between her breasts. Sucking the pink nipples into his mouth and scraping them with his teeth. Taking little nips. Sliding farther down so he could shower the same attention on her belly and the creases where thigh and hip met.

She writhed beneath him as he worked his way down once again to the sweetness of her sex between her thighs. Lifting her legs, he bent them at the knees to give himself better access and began stroking the wet folds of her sex with his tongue. He flicked the swollen nub of her clit and alternately tugged it with the edge of his teeth. Every time he did, Harper hitched her hips up toward him, sending little spasms through his cock.

He eased one finger into her, his shaft responding when he felt her inner muscles clench.

Jesus!

She was slick and hot, and her inner walls clamped down on his touch in a way that almost made him lose his control.

Another finger, spreading and stretching her, and then a third one.

Harper bent her knees and dug her heels into the bed, giving herself better leverage as she rode his touch.

He couldn't resist the need to lick that slick flesh and, when he did, she pushed even harder. God! She tasted so very sweet and blasted his taste buds with arrows of heat that went straight to his balls.

Balls, as a matter of fact, that were currently aching with need.

Grabbing the strip of condoms, he yanked one free and deftly rolled it onto his dick with one hand. Then, rising to his knees, he slipped his hands beneath the sweet cheeks of her ass, lifted her to him, and drove inside her.

Jesus!

She was hot and tight and wet, and he had to grit his teeth to keep from coming at that first grip of her inner muscles. His balls ached like mad, and his entire body was ready to combust. But then he gritted his teeth, braced himself, and began a steady in-and-out rhythm, the slickness of her walls dragging against the hard, swollen thickness of his cock. He increased his pace, a little at a time, until he couldn't hold back any longer.

He moved harder and faster, Harper's heels digging into the small of his back. Their rhythm increased until all he knew was her slick flesh, the heat of her, and the spasms of those inner muscles gripping him.

The orgasm hit them both at the same time, hard and strong, like the clenching of a fist over and over. She gripped him and milked him until he felt there was nothing left. As both their bodies went limp, he leaned forward, catching himself on his elbows and taking her mouth in a kiss filled with more emotion than he'd felt in a long time.

Finally it occurred to him he'd better get them cleaned up. He brushed another kiss on her mouth then told her to do nothing but lie there and he'd take care of her. As he climbed out of bed, it occurred to him that Ridge would be arriving soon to take the night shift, and he'd better not leave any telltale clues hanging out.

He disposed of the condom then allowed himself one more moment to lie next to Harper in bed before getting back to business.

"I should have told you," he said, "but I got distracted. Stone is sending Alex—Ridge—Ridgely—over to do night patrol so you and I can get some sleep." He glanced at his watch. "He should be here in about another thirty."

"What? Now you tell me?" She pushed at him. "Let me get up. I'll put on some coffee. Damn, Gabe. I have to make myself presentable."

He laughed, a low, hot sound.

"Any more presentable and I'd be fighting off the male population. But yes, we need to be presentable when Ridge gets here. I don't want you to be embarrassed."

"Living with wolves, nothing much embarrasses you after a while. But I want you to be comfortable." She tugged her bottom lip between her teeth. "Just so you know, I don't regret this one bit."

"Neither do I."

"And now I really have to get dressed."

"Meet you in the kitchen. And, Harper? Just so you know, this wasn't a once-and-done kind of thing."

Then he headed for the front of the building, afraid if he hung around, they'd be naked again when Ridge got here.

CHAPTER 6

RIDGE HADN'T OBJECTED when Stone asked him to take a night patrol assignment. He was actually a man who liked his solitude, and the preserve was a good place for someone like him. He liked the natural beauty of it… the towering lodgepole pines, white spruce, and Douglas firs along with lush juniper bushes and sagebrush. Especially in late summer, when the colors were bright just before they began to turn.

Stone had given him the code for the gate, so he punched it in, climbed out of his vehicle to close the gate behind him, and proceeded slowly the short distance to the building that housed the offices as well as Harper Young's living quarters. Stone Jacobs had already told him Gabe had pitched a tent to use, and since Ridge didn't know Harper, he headed for Gabe's setup first. The tent was pitched just a few feet from the office building and a lean-to that housed an ATV, but far enough away that Gabe still had his privacy.

But there didn't seem to be any signs of life in the tent, and the little fire pit Gabe had built showed no signs of life. Okay, he must be in the little building because he knew the man would not leave Harper Young unprotected. Swallowing a sigh, he climbed the two steps to the porch and knocked on the door. It was opened by Gabe, who motioned him to come in.

"Glad you're here," he told Ridge. "I don't trust those asshole cowboys not to make nighttime visits."

"No problem. I can use the brain exercise. And I like being out by myself at night."

"Come on in and meet Harper, and we'll give you all the background."

Gabe led him into the kitchen where the woman herself was just filling a coffee mug.

"Ridge Ridgely, meet Harper Young." Gabe nodded from one to the other. "And thanks for doing this."

"No problem."

She handed him the mug. "You'll need this for your night patrol, something to get you started. And thanks for doing this. I'm glad Stone realized we needed extra eyes at night, especially after the last couple of incidents. Oh, and I've also got a thermos I can fill for you."

"Much appreciated.

Ridge didn't know what he'd expected of Harper Young, but it wasn't what he saw. She certainly looked a lot more feminine than he'd expected of a woman who ran a wolf preserve. She was also one of the few women he'd ever met who managed not to need makeup. Her figure was not lacking, either, neatly wrapped in a T-shirt and worn jeans.

And were those vibes of some kind he caught between her and Gabe? Hell, the guy had only been on the assignment for two days. What would Stone say if there was monkey business going on?

He'd say mind your own business as long as the job gets done.

And that was the line he was sticking to. They were here for a purpose, and anything beyond that he had to trust his teammates to handle properly.

"Stone gave me a rough outline," he told Gabe, "but I'm hoping the two of you can fill in some details."

"Have a seat." Gabe gestured to the kitchen table. "I'll tell you what I know, but Harper has the most information. It's what sent her to Stone in the first place."

As they drank their coffee, she filled him in on the fact that cowboys from Ed Culhane's ranch were stalking her on the other side of the fence. That some wolves had been shot illegally. That so far she'd been shot at herself, twice, from the other side of the fence.

"I took these pictures today." Gabe scrolled through the photo app and handed over his phone when he'd found what he wanted. "I wanted to make sure these guys knew we were keeping an eye on them much like they wanted us to know they were doing."

"It's my understanding they want to shut down the preserve. That right?"

"It is." Harper nodded. "They want unrestricted hunting privileges as well as the opportunity to buy the land and add to their own holdings. Especially Ed Culhane who has the longest border to this property."

"What about the government regulations?" Ridge asked. "They're usually pretty strict, aren't they?"

"Yes, but Ed Culhane and his sidekick Frank Winslow have a lot of power and influence, especially when it comes to elections. No one wants to cross them."

Ridge took a swallow of his coffee.

"So we discovered. Stone sent us into West Yellowstone today to chat up the locals, and that's the story we got everywhere. Some people want to get rid of them and their influence, and others want to kiss their ass, but the word is they control just about everything. And most people just want to stay on their good side."

"If we can get something definitive on them," Harper told him, "we can put a real dent in their activities. So far, though, we haven't been able to."

"Let's see if we can catch them at something. I'm pretty good at that."

She'd put together a folder for Ridge that had a map of the preserve as well as some photos so he could see what the vast acreage looked like. She also had pictures of several of the wolves, racing from one place to another, posed on a small hill of rocks, or running in pairs.

"Like I told you—and I can't stress it enough—the wolves are nocturnal creatures," she told him, "most active at night. That's when they hunt, mate, and take care of other activities. They usually start in the early evening and go until dawn. Most of the time during the day they are sleeping."

"But you run tours here, right? Don't visitors want to see them?"

"They've learned to be curious, and we have enough sightings to keep visitors happy."

"Just move slowly," Gabe told him, "and they won't bother you. I've only traveled the property a couple of times, but I haven't had a problem.

"I marked where I usually see the ranch hands." Harper pointed to the dots on the map. "They hide in the stands of trees, but I've gotten good at spotting them. Especially after a few cut the fence a couple of times and I had to be extra vigilant."

"That would let the wolves out, right?"

"And allow the ranchers to shoot them. And shoot at me, which is how I ended up going to Stone in the first place."

"Well, if you'll fill up that thermos, I'll be on my way to do a little night crawling. I had plenty of practice with that over in the sandbox."

"Here's a two-way radio, also," she told him. "Anything wonky you think can't wait until you get back, call me. Just press the button, and it connects."

"I won't call except in an emergency. I don't want to wake you."

"It's okay. I'm paid to be awakened." She grinned.

Harper and Gabe walked him out to the lean-to and waited while he cranked the ATV engine. Then they watched him as he pulled away from the small building and headed out into the preserve.

The night was still and filled with the scent of the trees and shrubs. He drove slowly, taking in every detail of the land as he covered it. He'd been out ten minutes before he saw his first wolf. A pair of them, actually, climbing a rocky outcropping and staring straight at him. At least he figured they were from the way they stood. He put the engine into Park and waited to see if they'd head for him, but, after a few minutes, they turned and raced off in the opposite direction.

Okay, then.

Ridge drove slowly, remembering the night patrols over in the sandbox and the thick stillness of the air. This reminded him of it, the expectation of a hostile watching him from behind rocks or trees or, worse yet, taking a shot at him. He wondered if he'd encounter that tonight.

He'd driven for another fifteen minutes when his sharp hearing picked up a faint clomping sound from the other side of the fence. He stopped, putting the ATV in Park, took out his night-vision goggles, and peered past the fence between the preserve and the Culhane ranch.

There!

In a thick stand of trees, practically invisible without his NVGs, a man sat astride a horse, his posture erect, a rifle across his thighs. He held binoculars up to his eyes.

Okay, I can play this game, too.

Ridge sat for at least ten minutes, watching the other man, waiting to see who would blink first. He knew for sure it wasn't going to be him. Then he took his phone out of his pocket and fiddled with it. He'd spent the money for one that shot pictures in the dark as well as the light, and snapped off four images of the man.

The ranch hand never moved, but he did lower his binoculars. Then he took some pictures of his own. Ridge watched to see what the man did next, but before anything happened two more wolves came racing out of the trees and ran along the fence line. He hoped to fuck they didn't try to jump the fence and maybe impale themselves on the wire that ran along the top.

Or maybe come after him.

But then they turned and sprinted away in the opposite direction.

Ridge just stayed in the ATV, waiting to see whatever happened next. The ranch hand apparently decided he wasn't going to scare anyone off, and had probably been told no shooting tonight, because he shoved his rifle in the scabbard at the side of the saddle, nudged his horse with his heels, and trotted off away from the preserve.

Ridge waited until he was sure the man had gone before putting the ATV in gear and moving again. The night was thick with silence, broken only by the occasional howling of wolves and the sounds of other wildlife. He loved the solitude of being out here like this and had always volunteered for the night patrols. At least here he didn't have people shooting at him. He hoped. The ranch hand hadn't seemed interested in exchanging gunfire.

After another hour of crisscrossing the ground and checking different spots, he pulled into a stand of lodgepole pines and opened the thermos of coffee Harper had given him. Damn, but the woman made good coffee. He sipped slowly, taking in his surroundings, inhaling the night scents.

He wondered how Harper had gotten into this, anyway. And if something was going on between her and Gabe. He knew Gabe was a total professional and never made a mess by crossing a line. He assumed Harper was the same, or Stone would not have put this project together. Still, there had been something simmering in the air between them. Harper was what Ridge called "natural sexy," and he could see where Gabe would be attracted to her.

But he also knew Gabe and, from what little Stone had told him about the woman, he was pretty sure that even if they'd already heated the sheets, neither of them would do anything to jeopardize this situation.

Not my business, anyway.

But Gabe was a loner who hadn't accumulated any relationships. If it didn't jeopardize the situation, Ridge wouldn't mind if the man found a little comfort. Lord knew after what they'd been through, he certainly could use it. Being older than the others, with a tough life, Ridge considered himself a good judge of character, and he'd trust Gabe not to do anything to fuck this up, or piss Stone off.

He rode farther, enjoying the stillness of the

night and the absence of people. He had reached a far corner of the preserve, the place where the map indicated it butted up to Frank Winslow's ranch, and was about to grab another cup of coffee when he spotted something in a grove of white birch on the other side of the fence. Again, he pulled out his NVGs and focused on the man astride the horse. The man stared back at him.

Ridge decided he'd just sit here and see what the other man would do. Just as before, he sat there and watched Ridge. Okay, two could play this staring game.

But this time the man grabbed his rifle from his lap, wrapped his fingers around it, and took off away from the fence.

"Good move," Ridge muttered.

He waited until the man had disappeared then headed diagonally across the preserve. Although he was pretty sure neither of the ranch hands were about to shoot at him, he drove a zigzag pattern until he had covered most of the return. Nothing there.

He wanted to tell Gabe about the two armed ranch hands, but as things stood at the moment, he didn't think it was worth waking the man. He'd give him and Harper a full report in the morning when he clocked out. As long as no one was shooting at him, he wasn't shooting back.

He spent some time taking more pictures of the

preserve just so the others would have a feel for it and drove the entire fence line looking for more spies, but apparently they'd called it a night. Except for the two idiots, he'd enjoyed the darkness and solitude. He pulled into the lean-to and turned off the ATV ignition. The sun was coming up, and there was activity in Gabe's tent. In a moment, the man himself appeared. He looked sightly rumpled, but at least Ridge knew the man had gotten a good night's sleep.

"How'd you make out?" he asked Ridge.

"Good, good. But I do have a couple of things to report. Want to split the rest of this coffee with me?"

"No, thanks. The light's on in the kitchen, so Harper will have made fresh. Let me wash my face and hands, and we'll get some."

Harper not only had brewed a new pot of coffee, but she also had bacon sizzling in a pan and was scrambling eggs in a bowl.

"Nice of you to do this," he told her, "but not necessary."

"Oh, it absolutely is," she protested. "You guys are helping me out of a dangerous situation here. The least I can do is feed you."

Gabe helped her carry the plates to the table,. And when they were all seated, he looked at Ridge.

"Okay, give," he told Ridge. "I'd like to think you

had an uneventful night, but I have a feeling that's not the case."

"No, you're right." Ridge swallowed a bite of scrambled eggs and chased it with a gulp of coffee. "We had company last night."

"Ranch hands?" Harper asked.

Ridge nodded. "About two hours apart. First one was on Ed Culhane's side of the fence."

"Was he armed?" Gabe asked.

"He was. But he just sat in the trees watching, with a rifle across his thighs. Oh, and he had binoculars."

"Binoculars?" Harper stared at him. "I don't know what he was looking for because he knows I never—or almost never—go out at night, and I'm plainly visible when I'm out there."

"He wanted you—or whoever—to know he was watching you carefully."

"Damn."

"What did he do with the rifle?" Gabe asked.

"Left it lying across his thighs until the guy finally took off. I shot some pictures of him with my phone. I'm gonna send them to Stone and ask him to print them out. Pass them around to the others."

"And then what?" Gabe asked.

"We sat and stared at each other for a while. Then I guess he figured I wasn't about to be scared off, and I'm sure his orders were not to shoot, at least now, so he's gone."

"And that was it?"

Ridge shook his head. "No. I'd say around midnight, I saw another one on the land that you told me was Frank Winslow's, Harper. Same routine. Sat stride his horse, rifle at hand, doing nothing but staring. Got his picture, too."

"But what good does that do?" Harper wanted to know. "We're aware of where they're coming from. And I don't think they're stupid enough to shoot at me knowing you guys are around."

"I wouldn't take anything off the table," Gabe told her. "We'll see what Stone has to say. Maybe we need to get some of the others over here."

Ridge shook his head.

"Not necessary. I can handle it. I'm used to dodging bullets, and, if need be, I'm a better shot than anyone they can send our way. But I do want to fill Stone in."

Harper topped off the coffee mugs then Ridge called Stone.

"I'm sending you these photos," Ridge told him. "Make sure Stone gives copies to every-one. And let's see if we can track them in town, too. I don't want to leave anything to chance. I'm heading back to the lodge to catch a quick nap. I want Stone to send a couple of the guys into town to see if they hear any gossip. The ranch hands can't always keep their mouths shut."

GABE AND HARPER spent the morning together. She took care of paperwork then Gabe tagged along with her while she checked on the wolves and the other wildlife.

"I didn't realize wolves sleep so much during the day," he told Harper.

"Because they're nocturnal animals, when I do a night patrol, I monitor them carefully to make sure they aren't doing anything weird."

Harper insisted on riding the preserve with Gabe a second time, trying to quell the uneasy feeling she'd had since all of this started.

"I'll feel better if I check on things again and don't see any stray ranch hands spying on me."

"After last night, they may not want to," Gabe told her. "But let's be careful, all the same."

They didn't see anyone during the morning, but at noon, Stone called Gabe with some news. He put him on speaker phone so they could both hear.

"Gossip around here is Ed Culhane and Frank Winslow are hosting a barbecue and hunt next week for the men who buy cattle from them."

"Great." Harper blew out a breath. "Just what we need. The liquor flows freely, there's a lot of activity, and several of the guests think they're here for a wolf hunt."

"Are they?" Stone asked.

"Stone, you know they've gotten away with bending the rules before if they wanted to. Money talks and plenty of people have their pockets open. And that includes the number they can bag. Why would they think this is any different?"

"Because we're going to make it different," he told her. "Again, it's hunting season right now, for a limited time, and there's also a limit to the number of animals you can kill. But as I said, Montana lawmakers and Governor Greg Gianforte say wolves threaten the agriculture and hunting industries and passed sweeping changes in Montana game laws during the last legislative session. The new rules laid out in clear terms to the state fish and game commission make killing park wolves much easier and much more likely."

"But not in my preserve," Harper insisted. "Those animals are protected."

"Unless you get people sneaking over the fence or taking a part of it down or whatever."

"When is their rowdy crowd supposed to arrive?" she asked.

"Word is Ed's moved it up a week. He's got some people hot to trot to get sperm from his prize bull and a couple of ranchers who want to buy some of his herd. They made hunting a part of the deal, so he's hot to get on with it."

"Stone, what am I going to do? You know he's going to have his hands spying on me again, trying to scare me off."

"We'll handle it," he assured her. "I just want you to be prepared. "Meanwhile, Gabe is there twenty-four seven, and Ridge will be doing night patrols, so we'll have warning if anything starts to pop. We'll keep a lid on it, Harper. I promise."

"Okay, Stone. I trust you. That's why I came to you in the first place."

"And I'll take care of things."

Gabe ended the call.

"And he'll do it," he assured her. "Meanwhile, I'm going to take another turn around the preserve. It won't hurt things for Culhane and Winslow to see that I've got eyes on things."

"Be careful out there," she told him. "I've got more paperwork to do this afternoon, but then I'll make dinner. The least I can do is feed you well."

Gabe lifted her from her chair and pulled her against his body.

"That's the very least," he agreed. "I have something much better in mind for later."

She studied his eyes, searching for she didn't know what.

"Gabe, are we making a mistake here? We hardly know each other."

He brushed his mouth over hers.

"No mistake. Life doesn't always give you second chances. I was thinking last night I ended up here for reason, not only at Yellowstone but assigned to you. I think we could have something real here, Harper. Let's not let it get away from us."

"Things…don't always work out for me," she told him.

"They will this time. I promise." He took her mouth in a hungry kiss that sent shivers through her entire body.

"I'll take your word for it," she told him when he lifted his lips from hers.

"Let me get out on my patrol. Then we'll see if Stone had any luck reaching out to people about this hunt. After that, dinner and occupying our time until Ridge gets here."

CHAPTER 7

Ed Culhane leaned back in his desk chair, put his feet upon the desk, and his hands behind his head. "I'd say we're in good shape here," he told Frank Winslow.

Frank nodded. "Looks it to me. You still got plans for that woman? We need her out of the way."

"And she will be, one way or another. We've got fat pockets coming to this shindig, and, if they want to hunt wolves, I'm not letting any snippy-ass bitch put a limit on it."

"But the licensing board—"

"Is coming to the big barbecue, and they're all getting fat donations to their next campaigns. Will you relax? Anyway you know we have a plan B if we need it."

"A risky one," Frank reminded him.

"But we can use it if we have to. I've had your

men and mine tracking that bitch, so we know her routine, and we'll handle it if we need to."

"And that warrior type who's glued to her side?"

Ed snorted. "Hell. I can take a military guy with one hand. They all think they're hot shit."

"If you say so." Frank rubbed his neck. "I'm not happy about it, that's all."

"Would you be happy to see all that money walk away? You've got a fat pile of stud fees coming in if we can deliver on the hunt."

"No, and I do trust you. I can't help being nervous, is all."

"Let's go over the schedule once more," Ed told him, "so we've got it all fixed in our minds. And let's keep our eyes on her and her soldier boys, so we don't leave anything to chance."

HARPER DIDN'T EVER REMEMBER RUSHING through dinner and the dishes so fast. She wondered if Gabe was as turned on as she was, but one look at the heat flashing in his eyes was all the answer she needed.

What was she doing, anyway?

She'd had shallow relationships over the past few years, but nothing that gave her the same hot thrill or made her want more than being with

Gabe, and after only one night. What was going on here?

Something she didn't want to let go of, that was for sure.

When the dishes were finished, Gabe took her hand as if it was the most natural thing in the world and led her into the bedroom.

"You've had a busy day," he told her. "Me, too. I think a nice, hot shower is in order."

She let him lead her into the bathroom and reach in to turn on the shower. In seconds, the area was filled with steam. Gabe very slowly removed her clothes, lifting her T-shirt over her head and taking a long moment to stare at her breasts with a hungry look. She didn't recall a man ever looking at her with such heated desire blazing in his eyes.

He traced the curve of each plump breast above the edge of the bra before removing the piece of clothing itself. Then he leaned his head forward and traced the curves with his tongue, sending shivers racing down her spine.

Just as slowly, he unfastened her jeans and drew them down her legs, then her panties before helping her step out of everything.

"I think one of us still has too many clothes on," she told him in a shaky voice. She wondered that she could still talk as aroused as she was.

"I'd say it's time for you to return the favor," he

told her in a rich, deep voice. "But I don't think I can wait that long."

He was out of his clothing almost before she could blink, tossing them in a heap on the floor. Then he reached into the shower and tested the temperature of the water. Finally, he stepped into the enclosure and drew her in with him. The heat and humidity surrounded them at once, creating an erotic environment as their bodies connected from shoulders on down.

Harper had splurged on a rain showerhead, one of her few luxuries, so the water cascaded in a soft waterfall that instantly woke up every erogenous zone in her body.

"I've waited all day for this," Gabe murmured, cupping her cheeks and brushing his mouth against hers.

She opened her lips, and he slid his tongue inside in a wickedly erotic action, setting all her hormones ablaze and making the pulse between her legs come instantly to life. She squeezed her thighs together and pressed her body to Gabe's. In the small shower enclosure, it was easy enough to do.

Gabe lifted his mouth, reached for the body wash, and poured some into one of his palms.

"I thought about this all day," he told her. "Had a hard time keeping my dick in my jeans. Harper, I don't know what it is, but you turn me on more than any other woman I've ever been with. I could spend every minute doing nothing but making love to you."

"I feel the same way," she told him in a shaky voice. "This has never happened to me. You must have some kind of erotic mojo."

"Maybe just for you," he murmured and nipped the lobe of one ear.

Then he smoothed the thick lather over her body, starting at her shoulders and working his way slowly down her arms then over her breasts and down over the slight curve of her belly. Shivers raced over the slick surface of her skin, and the pulse between her thighs ramped up with a heavy rhythm.

I'm in big trouble here.

She clutched his shoulders to steady herself as he poured more body wash and worked it into the skin of her hips and upper thighs. Every brush of his fingers ignited more nerves and ramped up the pulse thudding between her legs.

She wanted to cry out when he stopped his stroking and caressing at her hips but then he turned her to face the shower wall and worked lather into her back. His fingers were magic, awakening every nerve and pulse in her body. When he slid his soapy fingers down the crease of her ass, she had to suck in a breath and clench her hands to keep from moaning. More shivers raced through her as he danced his fingers against her sensitive skin.

When he moved his fingers to grasp the cheeks of her ass and pull her tightly against him, pressing his shaft against her mound, she almost came just standing there. But Gabe knew exactly what he was doing, teasing her to the brink then backing off.

Finally, he turned her again, this time to face him. Then he poured more body wash into his palm, worked it into a lather, and stroked her mound and the lips of her sex. God! She never wanted him to stop. The beat of her pulse grew stronger, and she tried to squeeze her legs together against the constant throbbing. But Gabe lifted one leg, braced it over his hip, and slowly eased first two of his fingers inside her then added a third.

She was so aroused by then she came at once, the intensity accelerated when he used his thumb to tease her clit. She squeezed against his touch and clung to him as her body shook with pleasure. Gripping his shoulders, she held on for dear life as the spasms rocked her. When the last ripple died away, she leaned against him, spent and exhausted.

"You get to have all the fun," she murmured, forcing herself to take a step back from him.

She had to find a way to return the pleasure, though. To show him she shared the feelings, the desire. She took a deep breath, let it out slowly, and dropped to her knees. Shaking off his attempt to stop her, she took his thick, swollen cock into her mouth. She took her time lapping its length, running her mouth up and down the thickness and gently scraping it with her teeth.

"Christ have mercy," he groaned, his voice raw with passion and hunger.

Harper slowly licked and sucked, running her tongue up and down, sliding the thick shaft in and out of her mouth. He groaned when she reached one hand between his thighs to cup his balls and give them a gentle squeeze. She had never been this aggressive with a man before, but no man had ever affected her the way Gabe Walker did.

Oh, she was in big trouble here, but she didn't care. This might not last, but she was going to enjoy every minute to its fullest while it did.

She tightened her grip on his throbbing shaft, sucked harder, and squeezed his balls at the same time. He erupted into her mouth, bracing himself on the shower wall as moans burst from him. His body shook with the spasms until, finally, they slowed and then faded.

"Jesus, Harper." His voice was thick and rough. "You just do it to me."

Her lips curved in a smile. "Good. That was my intention."

"But now we have to take care of you."

She wanted to ask him how long he'd have to wait to do that, but he just drew her to her feet, braced one of her legs on a hip, and thrust three fingers inside her. She was already so aroused from his earlier touch that it barely took seconds before she felt the orgasm rumble up from inside her. All it took was for him to press his thumb against her clit, hard, and her orgasm burst from her, shaking her body.

Gabe pressed his mouth to hers in a hungry kiss, dancing his tongue with hers and coaxing her body to continue riding the orgasm. When the last shiver had faded, he kissed her mouth gently then turned off the shower.

"This is not just fun and games, Harper," he told her. "I know it's only two days, but sometimes, people make a connection that can last forever. I've been alone a long time, wondering if I'd ever find a woman I thought who could adjust to my lifestyle. I don't say stuff like this, ever. Ask Stone if you want to. But this hit hard, and I want you to know I'm not just playing games here."

"Me, either," she whispered, and realized she meant it. This happened so fast it scared her, but walking away from it would be even worse.

"Good. Good. When we take care of these assholes making your life miserable, we're going to take this somewhere. This is all new to me, Harper, and totally unexpected. I came out here to work with Stone, never dreaming I might find…this. But I'm not letting go of it. Count on it."

"I will," she told him. "Because I want it, too."

He cupped her face and gave her a kiss that scorched her down to the soles of her feet. But it was also filled with more emotion than she could have imagined. Then he opened the stall door and grabbed a towel.

"And now, we'd better get decent before Ridge gets here, or that guy is definitely going to suspect something."

"Let me dry my hair," she told him, "and I'll make coffee." She grinned. "And promise to behave."

"I think my military training will come in handy."

"I'd rather you use it to get these assholes off my back."

"That, too," he told her and combed his fingers through the wet stands of her hair.

She leaned against him for a long moment, absorbing his strength. Then she picked up her dryer. Time to get back to reality.

"WE HAVE two days until everyone gets here," Ed Culhane said.

They were at Frank's where they'd gone after dinner in town. Wining and dining the licensing people. The dinner was expensive, which would have been okay if they had gotten better results.

"We need a special release on permits, and I know they can find a way to do it. They can do anything."

"Maybe they can't get the governor to sign off on it," Frank suggested.

"With as much as we pump into his campaign," Ed pointed out, "he needs to dig deeper and find a way. How the hell do they expect us to keep that female off their backs otherwise? They haven't done such a good job themselves."

"It's a touchy situation," Frank reminded his friend. "If they're too heavy-handed about loosening the regs, even for short period of time, they'll get other organizations on their ass, and that will be a problem come election time."

"Fuck it all anyway." Ed blew a stream of smoke. "Why did we have to get some nature do-gooder here anyway? She's worse than all the others."

"Because Jim Haggerty was here forever, and she was his choice." Ed pulled a cigar from his pocket, clipped the end with special solid-gold clippers, lit up, and took a healthy drag. "We need to make her go away."

"Easier said than done," Frank pointed out.

"Maybe for a little while." Ed blew a perfect smoke ring. "So we can have our shindig, entertain our guests, and give them a chance to collect as many pelts as they want. Barbecue one day, hunt the next, and we're done."

"Within reason," Frank reminded him. "Go too far over the limit, and Miss Antsy Pants won't be the only one on your ass."

"Yeah, yeah, yeah." He took another draw on the cigar, blew another ring. "We really only need her out of the way until a day after the hunt."

"How exactly are you planning to do that, and what happens afterward? You know she'll run to the sheriff first thing. Or worse yet, those friends of Stone Jacobs' who look like they'd kill their neighbor while eating lunch. You make her disappear, and they'll be after your ass."

"They won't know anything," Ed assured him.

"And how do you plan to do that?"

"Think about it. We have the ideal place to stash her and make sure she doesn't see anyone. We release her when it's all over. She won't have seen anyone, including the men who grab her, or have any idea where they take her."

"Yeah? What place?"

"Think, Frank. What comes to mind. A place we haven't used for ages."

A smile broke out on Frank's face.

"Oh. Oh, yeah! Who will you get to do it, though? You gotta be careful here. They can't breathe a word to anyone. And they can't make a mistake and kill her, or all hell will really break loose."

"Smith and French. And she'll never see their faces, the way it will be set up. After two days, we release her. She can scream all she wants, but we'll release her far away from where we hold her, and what does she have to tell anyone. Nada."

"You'd better plan this down to the last detail," Frank warned.

"No, *we'd* better. You're in this, too. Remember. You're getting a stud fee and some extra goodies, too."

"I know, and I'm all in. We just can't make a mistake."

"I don't make mistakes. Now, sit down and let's plan this out. The crowd will be here day after tomorrow."

RIDGE ARRIVED as the sun was setting and accepted a mug of coffee from Harper. If he noticed anything about the two of them, he was careful not to show it. His reputation as a stone face was well earned.

"I have news," he told them, sitting at the kitchen table."

"Yeah?" Gabe lifted an eyebrow. "Let's have it."

"The guys were in town again today, doing their

tourist thing, although I told Stone they sure don't look like tourists to me."

"I think you're prejudiced," Gabe teased. "Anyway, let's have it."

"Apparently, Ed Culhane and Frank Winslow have this big shindig every year. They arrange to have their prize bulls stand at stud and collect a fortune for what's in the test tube. Dozens of people party and enjoy barbecue. Then the next day, they have a wolf hunt."

"We know about it," Harper told them. "But the licensing commission makes sure they stick to the limit and also the designated areas. They aren't allowed in Wolf World."

Ridge nodded. "And there's never been a problem before, as I understand it. But gossip on the street is some of these rich assholes have been pushing Culhane to get the limit increased and maybe even sneak them over here."

"I'm sure Stone's going to have the preserve well protected," Gabe said.

"Even so, if they decimate the wolf population, when Harper gets the okay to retrieve more animals, there won't be that many, and they'll be harder to catch. We get permission for a certain number each year, and it's already a complicated situation. "

"What about the governor and the commission?" Gabe asked. "They have rules to enforce."

"They also collect a lot of financial support for their political activities," Harper told them. "If they want to find a way around it, you know they will."

"We need to make sure the preserve is well guarded," Ridge said, "and no one can get in."

"That's why Stone is sending the rest of the guys. They'll be here first thing in the morning, and we'll lay out the plans. Meanwhile I'm doing night patrol tonight, and the others will be here tomorrow."

"I can't thank all of you enough," Harper told them.

If he'd been a few years younger and not poaching in a friend's territory, Ridge would have told her how she could thank him. But he was smarter than that and knew Harper and Gabe had already established a strong connection.

"We're fine," he assured her. "You can thank us when we're past this crisis and have something permanent set up."

He caught the look she and Gabe exchanged.

"Culhane isn't going to go away, and there are others like him. We're looking to set up a permanent security arrangement here."

"That would be...wonderful. Who, um, will that be?"

Ridge actually laughed, feeling the expression on his face soften a little. "I'll let you work that out with Stone, but my guess is he'll acknowledge that

Gabe is already familiar with the preserve and its operation. Don't quote me, though."

"What time does this disaster kick of?" Gabe asked.

"Culhane and Winslow host it annually, but word is it's bigger than ever this year. Also, with Harper in charge instead of Jim Haggerty, there's a renewed effort on their part to get rid of the preserve. Killing wolves is a good way to reduce the accessible population."

"Damn."

"Stone and the guys will be here in the morning to lay out the plans for security and protection. And now I'd better get going on my night rounds and make sure those jackasses don't try to pull stuff in the dark the way they do."

He let Harper fill his thermos for him, shook hands, and headed off to the ATV.

CHAPTER 8

As Ridge had told them, Stone arrived with the others at eight the next morning. He introduced Harper to Nate "Edge" Edgerton and Pierce, his German shepherd. To Wade Fielding and Justice Kane. They all shook her hand and, while they smiled, they all had a hard look on their faces that showed they were here for business. They'd all eaten breakfast at the lodge, but Harper made extra pots of coffee to fill everyone's thermos. It was a pleasant summer day with a moderate temperature, and the sun bathed everything with a golden hue. She noticed all the men checked their weapons and made sure they carried extra ammunition.

"I hope we aren't going to have a gun battle out there," Harper told Stone, frowning.

"So do I, but that's up to the idiots. Our job is

just to protect you and the preserve, and of course, the wolves themselves."

"Let's hope they don't think they are smarter than we are," Gabe said.

Stone laughed. "Don't hold your breath. What's important is we know we are."

They had driven over in two 4X4s, and they split themselves up between them and the ATV. Harper had printed out maps for everyone, so they could decide who would patrol what area. She had also included a list of instructions on how to behave around the wolves and other wildlife in the preserve.

"The wolves won't bother you if you don't bother them," she told everyone. "Gabe and Ridge can tell you what they've experienced, which might help. The important thing to concentrate on is the perimeter. Make sure no one has tried to cut into the fencing or found a way to climb over it. There's concertina wire in a couple of what I feel are the most vulnerable places. Spots where there are trees thick on both sides and someone determined enough could climb up, cut it, and climb over."

In only a little more time, she and Gabe and Ridge had everyone organized and ready to ride out. Ridge was going to sack out in Gabe's tent since he'd had night duty. And Justice, who would work with him tonight, would catch a quick one later, but for now, he wanted a daylight visual.

Harper would stay in the office, at everyone's insistence, and occupy herself with paperwork, of which she always had plenty.

"I don't need you out there making yourself a target until this mess is over," Gabe insisted.

She didn't know whether to laugh or cry. She wasn't used to someone being so possessive, but she had never felt so safe in her life. She wondered if any of the other team members had caught the intensity of the looks Gabe kept sending her way. And if they did, so what? Their connection was totally unexpected but she wanted to hang on to it.

She had canceled her two student helpers until Ed Culhane's big shindig was over and she was sure the danger of anything he might do had passed. The last thing she wanted to do was put them in harm's way.

So, paperwork it is, she thought, pulling a folder from the file holder on her desk. She had just sent everyone off, including Gabe, when her cell phone rang. She looked at the readout. Stone. And she had a feeling the news wasn't good.

"Culhane called off his party," she said, mentally crossing her fingers.

"Not even close," he told her. "In fact, my dad told me the crowd this year is the biggest one they've had. Ever."

"Maybe he'll be so busy with his guests he'll leave me alone," she told him.

"I'm worried he'll be even more anxious to give these people what they want, legal or not. And you stand right in his way. Do not leave your office, especially by yourself."

"Don't worry," she assured him. "I'm surrounded by the Army. I couldn't sneak out if I wanted to. And no deliveries this week except the mail, so we are good. Promise."

"Have Gabe call me when he finishes showing the rest of the guys around the preserve and getting people tucked away to stand guard duty."

"Will do," she assured him.

She worked through her stack of folders, lost in the quiet and forgetting about the disaster that might happen. Gabe should be returning soon, and she'd feel a lot better, even though she was locked away. She booked four tours, which made her feel good, and emailed information for several other groups.

She jumped at the sound when the buzzer for the gate sounded.

She pushed the speaker button.

"We're closed," she said into the mic on her desk.

"I guess I'll throw away the mail," a voice said. Paul, their mailman. Even he needed to be buzzed through.

She pushed the button and went back to her work. She was so engrossed, it didn't register when she heard footsteps coming in the back instead of up to the porch. Not until some kind of shroud was slipped over her head, drawn tight at the neck, and hands grasped her wrists.

Panic shot through her, and she struggled against whoever was doing this.

"Paul?" she squeaked.

"I'm so sorry, Harper." Paul's voice was ragged, as if he were in pain. "They threatened to shoot me. They—"

"Shut up," another voice growled. "Don't talk. Just shut the fuck up."

"But—"

Harper was trying to identify the other voice, but fear was coating her responses. Then she heard a thud. Before she could attempt to say anything else, the hood around her head tightened, and a needle pricked her arm. She tried to wriggle free as strong arms lifted her from her chair, but whatever was in the needle took effect at once.

And she fell into blackness.

GABE REALLY FLOORED the accelerator of the ATV after he left the other guys in place. Something was crawling up his spine that told him things were out of sync at the office. He'd called Harper, but when she didn't answer after three tries, his nerves sent him a big fat emergency message.

When he reached the office, he slammed on the brakes, leaped onto the porch, and barged into the office. What he saw made him sick to his stomach and sent fear plunging through him. A man with a US Postal Service shirt and cap lay unconscious on the floor in an uncomfortable position. Harper's work folders lay open on her desk, although some of them had fallen to the floor as if pushed there. And Harper was nowhere to be found.

"Harper!" He shouted her name then raced through the small building, but it was fruitless. She was nowhere to be found.

He called Stone at once.

"Emergency. Get over here now."

"What—?"

"Just get here."

Then he hung up and went about reviving the man.

The man's eyes fluttered open, and fear showed in them as he focused on Gabe.

"Don't hit me again. Please. I—"

"I'm not the one who hit you," he growled. "Did you see who it was? What the hell happened? Where's Harper?"

"They took her."

"Who? Who took her?" But he had a feeling he already knew.

He pulled himself together then helped the mailman to his feet and into the chair.

"They ran me off the road," the man told him. Then they pulled a gun on me and made me bring them into the preserve."

"Who, damn it? Who did this?"

"Two men wearing full-face hoods. I have no idea who they are."

But Gabe did, and it made him sick.

"You have to be buzzed through the gate, and that's what they wanted from me," the man went on.

"Where did they take her?" Gabe demanded.

"I don't know." The man held his head. "They didn't tell me anything. Just said to shut up and do what they asked or they'd shoot me."

Each of his team had radios with them that Stone had supplied, so he picked up his own instrument and pressed a button.

"The assholes have Harper. Stay at your posts. Stone's on his way. Be extra vigilant and observant and take note of anything you see. Anything at all."

"Ten-four" came from every instrument out in the field.

Gabe shoved his radio back on his belt and began to pace. He was glad Stone wasn't far away today. In less than fifteen minutes, he arrived, took one look at the mailman, and began cursing.

"Paul?" Then Stone turned his gaze on Gabe. "Okay, SITREP," he snapped.

"Two yahoos ran the mailman off the road and climbed in his van. They kept a gun on him so he would take them into the preserve with them, and when they got here, they put a hood on Harper, handcuffed her, drugged her, and carried her out of here. That's all I know."

"They have to be from either Culhane's or Winslow's ranch. I'd say Culhane's because he's the leader of the two and his ranch hands are nastier. I knew they were desperate to neutralize her, but I never thought even they would go this far."

"What's our next move? I told the guys to stay in position until you got here."

"Good." Stone nodded. "Give me your radio."

Gabe frowned but handed it over.

He pressed the button and said, "Everyone check in."

"Go for Kane."

"Go for Edgerton."

"Go for Ridgeley."

"Go for Fielding."

"Okay." Stone blew out a breath. "Gabe and I are going to hit both the Culhane and Winslow ranches. I'd say they most likely took her to Winslow's place, since Ed is hosting his big fucking party. But we'll hit both. I need you to watch for activity on the other side of the preserve fence. Part of it borders each ranch."

"You don't think they'd have her out in the open, do you?" Gabe asked.

"No, but we might spot some activity that will give us a clue. They can't just stick her out there on ranch property. Someone would see her. Plus, any of them could be called in to help if necessary."

"You don't think they'd have her at one of their houses?"

Stone shook his head. "Not everyone will be in on this, so they don't want people to see her. Especially the guests." He rubbed his jaw. "We need to figure out options. The first thing we need is a map of the entire area. Then we're going visiting."

They made sure Paul was okay to drive and threatened him with bodily harm if he breathed a word to anyone.

"But they'll hurt her," he protested. "You have to call the sheriff."

"We're a hell of a lot better than that sheriff," Stone assured him. "But we can't have the word getting out there. If they think there's danger for them, they'll kill her and make sure we never find the body."

Paul's face turned pale. "I-I don't want that to happen. I hate that they used me for this."

"You're lucky they didn't kill you," Stone told him. "Okay, Gabe. Let's go hunting."

Gabe's nerves were raw as they drove away from the preserve and headed for Ed Culhane's ranch. They passed through town and noted the increase in people shopping. Those not at Culhane's were out spending money.

They took the road that curved around from Ed's place on the other side of town. Even though the preserve and the ranch bordered each other, the roads came in from different directions, as was often the case out here.

Two men in jeans and Western shirts were manning the entrance gate at Culhane's, and they weren't eager to let Gabe and Stone onto the property.

"We don't let troublemakers in," one of them said.

"Then you'd both better quit," Gabe growled. "We just want to talk to Culhane for a minute." He paused. "About the extra license he asked for."

The taller man stared at him.

"You guys aren't from the licensing commission or the governor's office, so what do you have to do with them?"

"We'll tell Ed," Stone growled. "Now, unless you want to get fired, let us through."

Gabe could tell the men weren't the least bit happy about it, but they opened the gate and waved the two men onto the property.

The ranch stretched endlessly in two directions.

Gabe knew this amount of property had to cost a fucking fortune. No wonder Ed Culhane thought he had power to throw around.

As they got closer to the ranch house, he saw dozens of vehicles parked to one side and three helicopter sitting just beyond them.

"Money goes to money," Gabe said in a sarcastic tone. "Why drive a vehicle when you can take a helicopter?"

They managed to maneuver their way to the area next to the house and parked their vehicle on the grass. Finding Ed among the dozens of people mingled in two tents set up in the back yard was another problem. As they climbed out of Stone's vehicle, two cowboys approached them, each holding a clipboard.

"Names, please?" one of them asked.

"Not important," Stone said. "We just need a minute of Mr. Culhane's time."

The man lowered the clipboard and gave him a hard stare. "Sorry. This is a private party. Your name has to be on the list."

Gabe started to step forward, but Stone held him back.

"How about if you find Mr. Culhane and ask him to come here and chat? Tell him it's urgent."

The two men looked at each other, as if trying to decide what would get them in the least trouble.

Finally, the one who'd done the talking nodded his head.

"Wait here," he told them. "Hutch, don't let them move."

Hutch obviously took his orders seriously. He edged the two men to the side of the entrance to the tent and planted himself in front of them, one hand resting on the gun at his hip. Gabe and Stone stared right back at him until the other man returned with Culhane.

"What's this all about?" the ranch owner demanded. "Jacobs, you know you aren't welcome here. And who's your friend?"

"We're looking for Harper Young," Stone said, ignoring the questions. "We heard you wanted to talk to her and needed to find her first."

Culhane laughed, but there was no humor in it. "She's not welcome on this ranch, and neither are you or your friend. So, get the hell off my property before I have you arrested for trespassing."

"I don't think you want to do that," Gabe told him. "We'd have to bring in the sheriff, tell him we think Harper's somewhere here against her wishes, and ask him to tear the place up."

"Go ahead." Culhane shrugged. "I told you she's not here. Go ahead and call."

At that moment, Gabe knew wherever Harper was it wasn't here. Culhane was too eager for a search.

"Meanwhile," the rancher went on, "get the fuck off my property and don't come back. Now, excuse me. I have to attend to my guests."

"Let's go, Stone." He nudged the man. "If we don't find her, we can always come back."

"Don't plan on it." The man gave them a cold stare. "My men are armed and told to shoot intruders. Now, go away."

Gabe barely held it together until they were back in their vehicle, escorted by one of the armed ranch hands. As soon as their doors were closed, he started to say something, but Stone put a hand on his forearm.

"Not yet. Let's get off the ranch property first."

Gabe ground his teeth while they covered the long road from the ranch and turned onto the highway. After what seemed forever, his impatience got the best of him.

"You believe him when he said she's not here?"

"I do." Stone nodded. "He was willing for us to bring the sheriff. Regardless of any arrangement between the two of them, if he was willing for the sheriff to conduct a search, that's a good indication there's nothing to find."

"I don't trust him."

"Neither do I," Stone agreed, "but this time I believe him. We'll hit Winslow's ranch, but I'm betting she's not there, either. They've stash her someplace where no one can find her no matter how hard we look."

"So, you do believe he has her?" Gabe had a sick feeling.

"It's the only thing that makes sense. No one else would go to lengths like this."

"Then where is she?" Gabe demanded.

"That's what we're going to figure out, right after we take Winslow's ranch off the list."

CHAPTER 9

HARPER OPENED her eyes to darkness. Right, whoever had taken her had put a hood over her head so she couldn't see a thing. Fortunately, whatever drug they'd injected in her to knock her out hadn't been super effective—kind of like the drug she used on her wolves. The dosage only lasted a short time before the wolf woke up.

She didn't dare move. Anyone could be sitting nearby and would know in an instant she was awake. She didn't want to give herself away. So, she waited, and it didn't take long before the vehicle stopped. Big doors near her opened, allowing some light to cast through the bag's fabric. A big hand snagged her ankle and tugged her across a metal floor.

Wait. Had they put her in Paul's mail truck?

She couldn't struggle as she was carried then

dumped into another vehicle, the drug having left her woozy, and her lack of sight making the world spin. Was this how her wolves felt when they woke up? God she hoped not.

A trunk lid slammed closed over her. But somehow, she could still see light through her hood. Okay, so maybe this wasn't a car trunk, but maybe a car with a hatchback? Not that it mattered, she supposed.

The hatchback she'd been moved to was even more uncomfortable than the mail truck, and Harper's muscles were screaming for relief. On top of that, the floor in the rear of the vehicle was metal with no carpeting, and her butt was protesting madly. If she hadn't been so scared of what was happening, she might have focused more on her pains. But fear gripped her with an icy hand.

Where on earth were they taking her? And who were they? Were they going to kill her? She didn't think that was logical. Why not just kill her at the house? Why go to all this trouble and switching vehicles? Not to mention killing her would leave way too many questions in the aftermath. Maybe they were going to take her someplace far away to dump her, hoping she'd never find her way back.

She alternated between anger and fear. The only thing she was absolutely certain of was that in some way Ed Culhane was responsible for this. He was the only one with anything to gain.

They turned off the paved road and moved onto one bumpy enough she was convinced it was dirt. Not even gravel. She wracked her brain, trying to think of someplace on a dirt road where someone could be hidden, but there were too many abandoned buildings for her to even make a guess.

After what seemed like forever, they came to a stop but just briefly. One of them got out, as if to open a gate, then she heard him climb back in. What on earth? Now she had no idea at all where they were taking her. Was it a back entrance to Culhane's ranch? Or Frank Winslow's?

After a few more moments, they finally came to a stop. The engine was turned off, she heard doors open, and then the rear door was opened.

One of the men grabbed her by the ankles and pulled her forward. This time she fought him, kicking for all she was worth. She was pretty sure she landed a solid blow or two because the guy backed off.

"You want me to drug you up again?" he growled. "Got the needle right here."

She stilled. "No," she whispered.

"Didn't think so."

He latched on to her ankle and yanked her forward until her butt rested on the edge of the hatchback. Then he picked her up, threw her over his shoulder, and walked a few steps with her. There was no sound of gravel or heels on concrete, so she figured wherever they were it was dirt or grass all around them. She heard another door open, and then the man carrying her all but tossed her onto the floor.

"I want to see," she told him. "I want to know where we are."

"Where no one will ever find you."

In a minute, her hands were free and finally, *finally* the hood was removed from her head. She blinked against the shaft of light streaming in through two windows high on one wall, and sh rubbed her eyes with her fingers.

She looked up at the man, who still wore a ski mask over his face. She hadn't had time to pay much attention to him back at the preserve. Now she saw that he was tall and lean and dressed in typical ranch-hand wear.

"Where am I? Who are you? Why am I here? What do you want?"

"You ask too many questions," he told her. "You should mind your own business."

Why didn't the other man come in? Would she have recognized him, even with his face covered? She couldn't remember him from the brief glimpse she'd had of him. What was going on? She tamped down her fear and stared at the man again.

"I want to know your name," she demanded.

"What you want doesn't matter." He walked out, locking the door behind him.

"Wait!" she cried, scrambling after him. "Wait. Please. Tell me what you want."

In seconds, he was back, carrying a large paper bag. He opened it to show it held prepackaged ready-to-eat food."

"You won't starve. There's a bucket in the corner and bottles of water."

He turned to leave.

"Wait. Please," she cried again. "Why am I here? When can I leave? People will be looking for me."

"Trust me," he told her, "they won't find you here. Just be a good little bitch until this is over, and maybe we'll let you go home. See you tomorrow."

Tomorrow? How long were they planning on keeping her here?

But before she could ask him anything else, he walked out. The door closed, and a bolt slammed home on the other side.

Great. Just damn great.

Here she was, who knew where, with some kind of food and water and locked away from everyone and everything. She was pretty damn sure Gabe and the others would be hunting for her, but would they even know where to look?

There were two very narrow windows in the cabin, but they were high up on the battered wooden walls. Branches of trees thick with leaves blocked most of the light coming in. The windows were too high up for her to see out of anyway. And there was nothing for her to stand on.

The floor was also wood like the building, but solid planks that seemed indestructible. In the corner was a metal bucket. It didn't take much imagination to figure out what it was for. She had to fight the urge to throw up.

She spied a pile of rags in the corner and, when she checked them out she discovered it was a ragged sleeping bag. *Thanks for the comforts of home, guys.*

When she explored every inch of the place and realized with despair there was no way out unless those men allowed her to leave, she took a moment to indulge in a good cry, wiped her face on her T-shirt, and sat down with her back against one wall. She wouldn't let this defeat her. She was smart. She'd figure something out.

And there was Gabe, ex-Army Special Forces, her secret weapon.

God, she wanted to feel his touch again. Feel his hands on her and his body pressed against hers. Feel the thrill when he entered her, filled her, and drove them both to explosive orgasms.

Gabe would find where she was, one way or another. Until then, she'd put her own brain to work and see what she could come up with.

This had to do with Ed Culhane and the restrictions on hunting wolves. Today was his big annual shindig, and he was organizing a hunting party but she didn't think even he would go this far. Of course, when you had all the money in the world you tended to ignore rules and regulations and dispose of people who got in your way.

Well, not this time. Gabe and Stone and the others would find her and make the people who did this pay.

She wouldn't give up, no matter what. And then she'd get the governor and licensing commission to pay more attention to the situation with the wolves and the preserve. Meanwhile, it was time to think.

GABE SAT beside Stone as they drove down yet another long ranch driveway. This one was shorter than the other, the ranch house a little smaller, but the land stretched just as endlessly and small would have been a poor adjective to use. The ranch house itself was one story rather than two, but it sprawled in four directions.

There were no tents in the backyard, no party here, just horses in a corral and ranch hands attending to work. They parked in a graveled lot where three other vehicles already stood. Two ranch hands were already in front of them by the time they climbed out of their vehicle.

"We're not entertaining company today," the stocky one with brown hair said.

"Good," Stone told him. "Because we're not company. We're looking for someone. A woman named Harper Young. We think she might be here."

The two men looked at each other then shook their heads.

"Nope. Just us and the housekeeper. So, we won't keep you any longer."

"That's okay," Stone said. "We've got time. Frank around?"

"*Mr. Winslow*,"—he stressed the words—"is not here today. He's at an important event. And he doesn't have anyone here as a guest."

"Maybe she arrived and you didn't see her," Stone suggested, his voice deceptively mild. "A ranch this big keeps you pretty busy, I'd imagine."

"Not so busy we don't know what's going on," the man objected. "Why don't you give me your names. If someone shows up, I can get in touch with you."

"We can save you all that time and trouble if we can just take a peek," Stone said, his voice still in that nonthreatening tone.

But Gabe saw the muscles in his body tightening and knew Stone was getting ready to push.

He did not want to leave if there was a chance Harper had been stashed here away from all the festivities until everything was over.

At that moment, another man walked up from the corral. No doubt he'd been watching, and Gabe had the feeling he was more than a regular ranch hand.

"Problem?" He looked from Stone to Gabe to the ranch hands.

"Not at all." Stone's voice was back in that mildly deceptive tone. "We're looking for a friend of ours. We were told she's here, and we need to see her. And you are?"

"George Madison. Foreman." He did not hold out his hand. "And you two are…?"

"We already introduced ourselves. If we can just take a quick look and let our friend know we're here to pick her up, we'll—"

"There's no one here except regular hands. Mr. Winslow is hosting a big event at his friend's place. You can get going now."

Gabe looked at Stone. Although the other men were definitely hostile, they also did not act like they were hiding someone on the ranch.

"Fine." Stone looked at Gabe. "We'll keep checking other places she might be. We can touch base here again if we don't find her."

"That won't be necessary," Madison told him. "We're not expecting any company, so y'all can leave now."

"They know where she is," Gabe spat out the minute they were back in the SUV. "I could tell by the attitude at both places. Culhane and Winslow have her someplace, and they've given orders not to allow strangers on the ranch. But damn it, Stone. My senses just tell me if she's not here or at Culhane's, but they know where she is."

"I agree. What we need to do now is gather everyone together, including my dad, and study a map of the county to see what might be likely."

"The county!" Gabe practically shouted the words. "Fucking shit. Where the hell would we even start."

"With my dad, as I told you. There's nothing about this county he doesn't know, including every hidey hole or the possibility of one. Let's get back to the preserve, and we'll get him over there."

Gabe had managed to hold himself together while they'd gone to the ranches but he was getting to the end of his rope. It shocked him that Harper had come to mean so much to him in just two short days, but he'd had friends tell him before about it happening to them. They meshed perfectly. She knew his background in the military, he knew hers with the wolves, and he believed that when he wasn't on an assignment for Stone he could be of help to her. Regardless of what happened with this situation, there would always be people trying to shut her down, and he could be her backstop in that area, along with both Jacobs' men.

Stone seemed to know Gabe was not in the

mood for talking, unless you counted cursing, so they were mostly silent on their way back to the preserve. They had left Ridge in the office when they went out on their search, and he was sitting on the porch, a rifle resting on his thighs, leaning back in his chair but every muscle still on alert. As soon as the men climbed out of the SUV, he rose lithely to his feet and came forward, rifle pointed downward.

"Well?" he asked. "I'm assuming since it's just the two of you that you had no luck finding Harper?"

"Fuck, no," Gabe snapped. "The guys who work for those assholes swear there's no woman in either house, and the worst part is, I believe them."

"My dad should be here any minute," Stone said. "I told him to bring every county map he's got, digital and paper. We have to identify logical places they could stash Harper without calling attention to it."

"We called enough attention when we went to the ranches." Gabe snorted.

"Which is what I wanted. Maybe one of the hands—or more than one—is involved and will decide it's more than he wants to be part of. If nothing else, we put everyone on notice. We aren't quitting until we find Harper and take care of the assholes who grabbed her."

They turned as a four-door pickup pulled

through the gate and down the road to the little building. Gabe's father obviously had the code for the gate, which made things easier. He walked over to where the men were standing, carrying a tablet and a pile of folded maps.

"Let's go inside," John Jacobs told them. "We can spread these out on the kitchen table. Stone, we'll leave two of these guys here to patrol the preserve. I need Justice for what I have in mind."

"Nate," Stone told "Edge" Edgerton, "you and Pierce stay out there. Split the preserve between you guys. That dog will for sure keep people from trying to sneak in. You and Ridge split up the preserve and each take half. Ridge, you've already become familiar with the reserve. If you need gas, there's a big tank next to the lean-to. Constant patrols and continuous check-ins with each other. Keep your cells on so I can keep you up to date from this end. "

"Ten four," Edge told him.

Ridge echoed the acknowledgement.

John turned to Gabe. "You and Wade are with me. We need to look at the maps and figure out who goes where, but I've got an idea that may streamline that."

"Yeah?" Gabe snapped. "Tell me what it is."

"As soon as we identify the areas we need to search. Let's get to it."

Gabe unlocked the office door and led them all

into the kitchen. John Jacobs opened each map, smoothed it out then stacked them one on top of the other. Finally, he pulled out black magic markers from a pocket and dropped them in the middle of the pile.

"Okay," John said. "Let's get to it. We're looking for the most out-of-the-way places those assholes have access to that no one would think of. We'll circle each one then tack them up on the wall to see if there's a pattern before we go running off like a bunch of wild hares."

"Sounds good." Stone nodded.

Gabe could hardly speak from gritting his teeth, but he took his place with the maps. Since the Jacobs men knew the area better than any of them, he insisted they have first crack at it. When they found a place, even an unlikely one, he circled it, and Wade tacked the map up on the wall. They'd been through two of them when Justice rolled in, and John told him what to do.

Thirty minutes later, with John's guidance, they had all the maps on the wall and ten different places marked as possibilities.

"It will take us forever to hit every one of these," Gabe growled, "even if we split them up. And at least one of us has to stay here at the preserve in case one of those idiots decides with Harper gone they can cut the fence and let some of the wolves out to be hunted."

John nodded. "A good possibility. Okay, let's get a county-wide map and mark these spots on them to see if they have any relation to each other or to Culhane or Winslow."

He tapped his tablet to open it, pulled up a county-wide map, and began marking the spots they'd identified. Finally, John scratched his neck. "Covering all these on the ground will take hours, even with so many of us doing it. We need more help, and I have just the guy who can give it to us. Anyone up for a helicopter ride?"

HARPER PACED the shack for what seemed the hundredth time. Sitting on the floor made her butt get numb, and there was nothing else to use. Besides, she needed to keep her blood circulating.

Surely by now Gabe would have discovered her missing and rounded up the troops. She was sure he'd call Stone who'd maybe even pull his father into this. After all, he knew the county the best and could probably put a search together better than anyone else. Except she was in what she believed was such a godforsaken place no one would ever find it.

And her wolves. The thought of them being let loose and hunted made her sick to her stomach. She'd worked so hard to protect them, to keep them safe, to create an awareness of them. It could all be destroyed by those selfish bastards. She wanted to just cry, but she'd allowed herself enough tears already.

There had to be some way out of here for her.

Think, Harper.

Maybe if her captor came back by himself she could kick him in the balls, run out of here, and take off in whatever transportation he was using.

Yeah, right. Like he'd put himself in that position. He'd never get close enough to allow her the opportunity to do that. There were no stray pieces of wood in the shack she could hit him with, and he was twice as big and twice as strong as she was.

Damn!

If she got out of this—no, *when* she got out of this—she was going right to the governor to have these men punished and get him to pay more attention to the preserve and what it meant. They drew tourists to Yellowstone, which meant money for other businesses, and the more successful the preserve was the bigger the crowds.

Gabe's image flashed into her mind again. She known him less than three days but the connection they'd made shocked her. She hadn't seen herself with a partner of any kind, and certainly nobody had come along before this who interested her much. But Gabe…Gabe was different. In her mind, she already had them living together, with him working the preserve with her except when he had to take assignments from Stone. Which, after all, was his main reason for moving here. To keep working with his team.

She just hoped he felt the same way, and she wasn't fooling herself. A relationship needed more than off-the-charts sex to succeed. But…it was a necessary ingredient, plus they'd connected right away.

You can make it work, Harper. You know you can.

She wished to hell she knew where this cabin was. It might give her some idea of how to get out of this, although she didn't know exactly what that would be.

She kept pacing, counting her steps to keep her from losing her mind. It had to be someplace where either Culhane or Winslow had easy access, and her money was on Culhane. He owned the most property and had the biggest ranch. But his ranch was ten thousand acres. It could be anywhere.

Think, Harper. Think, think, think.

But no matter how she tried, how she pushed her brain, nothing came to her. She wanted to scream. She decided to calm down she'd go back to thinking of ways she could incapacitate her captor enough to get by him and to whatever vehicle he arrived in.

Something would come to her. It just had to. The fact she knew Gabe was probably turning over every stone in Yellowstone to find her gave her the strength she needed to keep going.

~

THEIR MOTTO at Fort Drum had been "Find a way or make one," and this was no exception to their rule. They needed to find Harper before Culhane and Winslow ran roughshod over regulations, wolves were poached, and Harper was harmed in some way. This was a disaster in the making, the result of egos so big they were dangerous.

"You know I'm a helo pilot," Justice told them. "Get me a chopper, and I'll fly anyplace."

John nodded. "I have just the solution. Santi Vincent is a self-made millionaire who, unlike many people, has decided giving back is where it's at. He owns two choppers and provides services for free. We've used him for search and rescue, medical emergencies, deliveries, almost anything you can name. I'm going to give him a call, Justice, and put you on the phone with him. Give him your creds, find out about his choppers, and then we'll get you to his place. It's not far from here."

"He doesn't charge?" Gabe asked. "Not that it would be a problem."

"He doesn't need the bucks. Years ago, he lost his fiancée because there was no medevac available. He decided to use his money for something in addition to making more money and does this for free whenever there's a need."

"Sounds like a hell of a guy," Wade put in.

"He is. Let me get in touch with him."

Gabe paced nervously while John put in the call. Every minute they weren't actively looking was another minute Harper was in danger. Every step he paced, every second that went by made it more obvious to him just how important this woman had become in such a short period of time. If anything happened to her…

"Yeah, that's the story, Santi. I'm pretty sure they stuck to this side of the county. We marked off a few places, but it will take forever to drive to each of them, and time is critical. We don't think they'll kill her, but that's not a given. You never know what will set off these maniacs. Uh-huh. Uh-huh. Yeah. We'll head to your place as soon as I hang up and work out the details then. Thanks, Sant. We'll owe you big time."

"He'll do it?" Gabe asked, each word lined with tension.

"Yes." John nodded. "He's about twenty minutes from here. We'll head to his place right now. Justice, you and he can decide who'll fly what, but it will be a big help having two of you up in the air."

Gabe thanked the military discipline that allowed him to ride the short distance without exploding. He'd never forgive himself if anything happened to Harper. In a little more than forty-eight hours she'd become the most important person in his life. He hoped to hell she felt the same way about him. He wanted them to have the chance to take this thing between them where he was damn sure it was going.

It was twenty minutes almost to the second when the caravan of three cars turned off the three-lane highway and drove down a long driveway onto property bordered by a split-rail fence. A large farmhouse that had obviously been renovated stood to one side, and beyond it a helipad fronted a large hanger with its doors open. Painted on the side were the words *Lone Wolf Aviation*. Gabe thought it an appropriate name for this situation.

As they pulled into the parking area, a man walked out to greet them.

"Thanks for doing this," John told him. "It's much appreciated."

"Hey. No one knows more than I do the value of a chopper in an emergency."

He shook hands with each of the men. Gabe noticed he was tall and lean, obviously in good condition. He had a square jaw, dark-brown eyes and brown hair silvering at the temples. In those eyes Gabe saw a wealth of misery that had been obviously lying there for years.

John introduced everyone and told him Justice would be the second pilot.

"I've got a Sikorsky S-76 and a Bell 428," he told Justice. "Let me check you out on both of them, and then we'll' decide who'll take which one. John, you said you've got maps? Let's go into the hangar and have a look."

Gabe wanted to scream at them to get going, but he knew unless they prepared well enough their chances of finding Harper were slim to none.

There was a long table against one wall where they spread out the maps, the condensed one as well as the individual ones. Santi weighed them down at the corners with rocks, and they went over each one.

"You can eliminate these two spots." He pointed to the areas. "There's no place to hide anyone, and too much traffic goes down those narrow roads. Tourists who like to get off the beaten path." He pushed them away. "But here, here, and here"—he pointed—"are good possibilities. Okay, let me get Justice here checked out, and we'll divide these up."

Gabe barely kept his impatience in check while they went through their routine until Santi was satisfied Justice was qualified to fly one of his heli-copters. Then they split up the maps. Santi would fly the Bell, Justice the Sikorsky since it was what he flew most of the time. They each took their maps, and Stone and Wade followed Justice to the

Sikorsky while Gabe headed to the Bell 429 with Santi Vincent.

"I can't tell you how much we appreciate this," he told the man as they buckled into their seats.

"You don't have to. I've been where you are before. My situation didn't have a very happy ending, but I'm going to do everything in my power to make sure yours does. Now, get your maps organized while I call the tower at West Yellowstone."

"Will Culhane or Winslow find out? Will they realize you're helping us in our search?"

Santi shook his head. "They're too busy being obnoxious rich bastards with their guests. Besides, it will never occur to them that such a full-out search will be mounted for a woman they consider insignificant and a pain in the ass."

"I'll show them insignificant after this is over."

"Insignificant being the operative word. Okay, let's get this bird in the air then give me the coordinates of the first site you have marked."

CHAPTER 10

F RANK W INSLOW DISCONNECTED the call on his cell phone and went to find Ed, who was in a corner of the tent chatting with two of the men who had come specifically for the wolf hunt.

"Excuse me," he butted in. "I hate to interrupt, but can you give us a minute? I need Ed for just a few."

The other men nodded although they made no effort to conceal the annoyance that flitted across their faces.

"What the fuck?" Ed snapped when they were outside the tent and away from other people.

"You've been playing footsie with the hunters this afternoon, so you weren't available when Stone Jacobs and another guy showed up looking for a woman they said was here. You know they meant that Young woman."

Ed's eyes bugged out. "And no one told me?"

"Did you hear what I said? You were in a tight conversation with two high rollers, and they didn't want to interrupt you."

"But you're telling me now?"

Frank nodded. "Because they went to my place looking for her, too."

"Shit. Damn it all. That woman is nothing but trouble. We should have buried her someplace where no one will ever find her. At least not until the next century."

"And that would have generated an even bigger manhunt," Frank pointed out. "This way, when we let her loose, she hasn't seen anyone to identify them or even have an idea where we've been keeping her."

"We'd damn sure better keep it that way. You think they'll be back?"

Frank shrugged. "Maybe. Maybe not. But the point is, we should let them search both houses if they show up again. They'll find nothing, and that will get them off our case."

"And when we finally let her loose?"

"Just like you said when we planned this. Middle of the night on a country road she's never been on before. She'll have no idea about anything."

"All right. All right. All right. I'll talk to my men. You talk to yours. I want to know pronto if anyone shows up at either house again."

"Of course. Meanwhile, I need to make sure tomorrow's hunt is organized."

THEY WERE twenty minutes into their search, and Gabe was ready to jump out of his skin. They had checked the first place on the map, landing the chopper and walking all around the designated area. It was an abandoned cabin that appeared deserted. It sat in a corner of what Santi told him was property recently foreclosed on.

"You think they'd take her to a place owned by someone else?"

"I think it fits the bill because no one ever comes here. The owners just walked away from it and live somewhere in Bozeman now. There's no caretaker for something that's just a cabin, and the chances of them being discovered are slim to none."

Their search turned up nothing, frustrating the hell out of Gabe even as he knew they had to search every inch to make sure. Now they were back up in the air and on to the next place.

Santi tapped Gabe on the arm and pointed below to another deserted cabin, this one partially shielded by trees.

"That place is too exposed, which is why it probably didn't make the map, but I'm going to check it out anyway. It fits the bill in everything else."

"Good. We can't overlook anything."

But again, they came up empty.

"John and Stone did a good job finding isolated places that people don't pay attention to anymore," Santi told Gabe. "They needed someplace away from everything, where nobody has been for ages or is likely to go. Someplace that if the sheriff were running a search he wouldn't think to look."

"Speaking of which, how come the sheriff isn't involved at all. Is he as crooked as these guys?"

Santi shook his head. "Not at all. Oh, he likes the money he gets at election time, but he wouldn't overlook something like this. No, if we got him involved with this, word would spread like a prairie wildfire, and they'd be convinced their only solution was to get rid of Miss Young permanently."

Nausea surged through Gabe, and he had to swallow it back hard. "Fuck."

"Exactly. Okay, read me the coordinates for the next spot, and we'll head to it."

"And you're sure we only need to check deserted spots?"

Santi nodded. "Places where there is no chance of them being seen at all. These guys are arrogant, but they aren't stupid."

"They are if they think they can get away with this."

Santi chuckled. "I'll agree to that."

By the time they hit the fourth spot Stone and John had marked, Gabe was about to lose his mind. His imagination was running wild, and he pictured Harper in all kinds of dangerous situations.

"I hope wherever she is there aren't any wild animals," he told Santi.

"That would be a poor decision on their part. They need her scared shitless but unharmed. Above everything, they have to have plausible deniability, and so do their men. If she's attacked by wild animals, whoever finds her body will report it. The sheriff will open an investigation, and all hell will break loose."

"True." He had to keep remembering that. "I just keep…"

"Imagining things," Santi finished for him. "That's natural, but you Special Forces guys have a lot of discipline. I know it's different when it's personal, but now is the time to call on all that discipline."

Gabe knew he was right. Time to get his shit together. While Santi checked in with Justice, he pulled the next map to the top of the pile. When Santi was finished, Gabe called out coordinates. The helo banked away to the left, made a turn, and headed north.

I'm coming, Harper. Wherever you are, hold on.

⁓

"This is some shindig. I gotta hand it to you."

A tall man with a slightly rounded belly and thick gray hair walked up to Ed Culhane.

"Thanks. We aim to please."

"Everything set for tomorrow?"

Culhane nodded.

"The vet will be here at ten to draw the semen from the different bulls. We'll store it in a special container until you're ready to leave. And the hunt starts at noon."

"I have to say, with all the regs the state has put in place, I don't know how you arranged a hunt with such loose regs."

Culhane laughed. "It isn't what you know, it's who. Right? Don't worry about a thing. You just write me that big fat check tomorrow for the draw and we'll all be happy."

"Not a problem."

Culhane hoped everyone felt that way. He was standing three bulls at stud tomorrow, which would net him a cool four million dollars. Life didn't get much better than that. It gave him enough money to buy his way out of whatever fallout there might be from the wolf hunt.

"Someone getting nervous?"

Culhane had heard Frank Winslow come up next to him.

"Nothing I didn't handle. After tomorrow, we'll be good as gold anyway. You have your two bulls ready to stand for the draw tomorrow?"

Winslow nodded. "And the buyers have their certified checks with them. It doesn't get much better than this, right?"

"Amen to that. I'm sending the boys out right after midnight to cut the fence. I had a guy teach them how to draw the wolves out, so we should be good to go. I told my hunters any wolf on my property will be fair game."

"I just hope this works." Frank frowned. "I just know Stone Jacobs and his boys are out hunting for the Young woman."

"So what? They don't have a clue where to look or who to ask. They won't come after us no matter how convinced they are we know where she is."

"And your men know to keep their mouths shut, right?"

Ed snorted. "I can't believe you even asked me that question. They talk, they'll be the ones going to jail. Keep that in mind."

"Just covering my bases. Kidnapping's never been in our bag of tricks before."

"And probably won't be again. But this event has brought you and me a total of five million dollars because of that wolf hunt. You can't tell me you'd turn your back on that."

"No." Frank let out a heavy sigh. "I'm just not eager to do it again."

"We probably won't have to. This most likely has scared the shit out of that woman and if we're lucky we can run her out of town. Get them to close the preserve and change the rules. The governor's going to be fundraising for a campaign soon . Keep that in mind."

"I'll do that."

"Okay. Let's get back to our guests. This is one party I'm really enjoying."

"I NEVER THOUGHT I'd fall in love."

Gabe's voice was deep and rough in her ear.

"Me, either." She gave a soft little laugh. "I thought it would be me and the wolves for the rest of my life. What man would want that kind of life?"

"I actually think the wolves are kind of sexy." Gabe smiled and nuzzled her ear. "Not as sexy as you, of course."

He nibbled her earlobe and smoothed little kisses along her jawline. Her entire body responded, despite the fact he'd just taken her to an explosive orgasm.

"I think you're pretty sexy yourself," she told him.

He slid one of his hands along the length of her thigh and her hip and up to where he could cup one of her breasts. When he pinched the nipple, even though it was sore from his tugging and pulling with his mouth, heat streaked through her.

She ran her hand over his thigh and to where his cock nestled in the thickness of a nest of hair. How on earth did she ever take all that inside her? No, the better question was, how was she lucky enough to end up with a man like Gabe? He was everything she'd ever wanted and never thought she'd have.

And he even loved the wolves!

She reached over to pull him closer to her and...

Banged her head against the wooden wall.

Damn!

She sat up and rubbed her head. She had just leaned against the wall for a minute, so tired from pacing the shack and wondering if she'd get out of this alive. And how was it that, in the midst of all this danger, she was having erotic dreams about Gabe Walker.

Because he's the one you've been waiting for without even knowing you were waiting.

What a dramatic and drastic turn her life had taken in just over forty-eight hours. And if she ever wanted to see Gabe again, she'd better figure out how to get herself out of this because she didn't trust whoever this was to actually set her free.

She began pacing again, running her hands over the walls, looking for any weakness in the wood, but there was nothing. How was it that a piece of junk like this shack could be so impenetrable?

Next, she went back to the door itself. Although there was a slide lock on the inside, she'd learned when her captor left there was one on the outside, too. But maybe if she could get something into where the door and the wall joined…That was the only place she found a sliver of space.

She grabbed the tattered sleeping bag to have something to hold on to, and, when she shook it, out some shards of wood fell to the floor. Had whoever this was captured someone else before, and they had tried to get out? But where? She'd found no chinks, but maybe these would help.

Grabbing one of the larger pieces, she worked to jam it where the door and the wall met and began trying to work it through. Her only hope was to be able to release the bolt from the other side.

Yeah, and maybe pigs will fly.

But she had no alternative, and she wasn't about to just die in here.

THE HELOS HAD BEEN UP in the air for close to an hour. Santi told them they each had five hours of fuel, so they were good for a long time, and Gabe wasn't about to land, or actually let Santi or Justice land, until they'd found Harper. He was getting more and more discouraged though as time passed.

They had checked out every spot marked on the maps, even landing near some of the more likely hiding places to search on foot, but with no results.

"I think they'd be foolish to do this," Santi said as they took off yet again, "but I think we should do at least a flyover at the Culhane and Winslow ranches. They have hundreds of acres with nothing but open range and thick clusters of trees. Maybe there's something there we don't know about."

"I'll try anything," Gabe told him, "although they'd be pretty damn stupid to hide her on their own property. Either of them."

"Except it would eliminate the chance of someone finding her. Let's give it a shot."

Santi radioed Justice to tell him what they planned to do and asked the other man to check the Winslow place while they took Culhane's ranch. Santi flew to the farthest corner and started from there. Gabe kept the binoculars to his eyes as Santi zigzagged back and forth over the vast property. They avoided the open spaces where there was no place to conceal someone and concentrated on the heavily wooded areas.

"But if they left her out there," Gabe pointed out, "she's subject to the weather. Would they want to take that chance?"

"Truth be told," Santi answered, "I don't know what the fuck they'd do. I never thought kidnapping someone to set up an unlimited wolf hunt would occur to them, but they do have a feeling of entitlement. They've gotten away with so much for so long, I guess they figured they could just buy their way out of it like they always did. I just…"

Suddenly, he banked the helo and flew over the area they'd just covered.

"Focus the binocs on that big thick grove of trees just below us. Do you see the hint of a cabin there?"

Gabe tried not to let himself get excited as he did what the man asked.

Yes!

Yes, there was the hint of a small building buried in the trees.

"I bet it's an old line shack," Santi said. "I'm going to land so we can check it out."

But as Santi banked the chopper, looking for the closest place to land, they saw a truck bouncing over the land, heading right for the grove.

"That's gotta be whoever is keeping an eye on her," Gabe said, trying to control his excitement. "God, I hope they haven't decided it would be easier just to kill her."

"Anything is possible, but I don't think they want a body to hide. And my guess is it's one of the hands. They probably blindfolded her so she couldn't identify anyone."

"The mailman said the two guys wore masks."

"Smart. Okay, I'm going back up. You keep those binoculars trained on the guy."

But he didn't have to tell that to Gabe, who was already focusing.

THE MAN CLIMBED out of the trunk, walked around to the other side, and pulled a bag from the passenger seat. Sliding open the thick bolt he'd installed before grabbing the woman, he pulled the door open...and had to throw up his arm as she flew at him and tried to claw the mask off he was wearing. She didn't succeed, but he felt her nails through the fabric and knew he'd have some scratches. Culhane would pay dearly for those, and for dumping this assignment on him.

"Watch it, bitch."

He grabbed her by both arms and shoved her away from him. When she tried to come at him again, he backhanded her, and she fell to the floor.

"Now just stay there and we'll be fine. I've got food and water in this bag, which I'm sure you want, so just stay where you are."

He set the bag as far away from her as he could and backed up to the door. As he started to open it again, he heard the drone of a helicopter.

What the fuck?

He backed out of the shack, slammed the door

shut, and bolted it then looked up in the sky. Sure enough, a chopper was flying overhead but away from this spot. Must be that rich fucking millionaire. He'd better not be looking for the woman. But then, why would he? She was nothing to him.

Still…

He pulled out his cell and punched in Culhane's number.

"We may or may not have a problem." He relayed the information about the helo.

"I can't imagine a guy like Santi Vincent would get involved in this, but let's not take chances. Stay hidden in the trees until he's farther away and heading in the other direction from where you are. Make sure the bitch is locked up tight. Then get back here."

"Will do."

He could hear the woman banging on the door and yelling something at him, but he tuned it out as he scanned overhead to watch the chopper. When he was satisfied they were definitely heading in another direction, he started the truck and pulled out of the thick grove of trees.

"He's gone," Gabe said, binoculars still glued to his eyes.

"Let's give it a few more minutes, so he's far

enough away and convinced we're no threat. Then we'll come in from the other direction."

It took all of Gabe's discipline to just sit there, watching, and not shout at Santi to land the damn chopper. Finally, when he was satisfied the man in the truck was no longer a danger, he did two things.

First, he called the other helo to talk to Stone and tell him what they'd found.

"That ranch is so big," he said, "he's got a long ways to go to get back to the main house. Find him, land so you block him, and grab him. He's our next weapon."

"Will do," Stone assured him. "You guys go and retrieve Harper."

Santi landed on a flat area right outside the grove of trees. After checking their guns, they raced through the tall lodgepole pines until they reached the cabin.

"Door's bolted," Gabe said, "but from the outside. Assholes."

He slid the bolt to the side and yanked the door open, to be greeted by a furious woman reaching to claw his face.

"Hey, hey, hey!" He grabbed her wrists. "It's me. Gabe. I'm the good guy, remember?"

She stared up at him with wild eyes then collapsed against his chest. She was shaking, and her hands were scraped where she'd obviously tried to find a way to reach the outside bolt. She threw herself into Gabe's arms and clung to him as if she'd never let go.

"It's okay. You're safe now. We've got you, and we have eyes on the bug holding you prisoner. God." He held her tightly. "I thought I'd never find you."

"Let's get her the hell out of here," Santi said, "in case that jerkoff decides to come back."

Santi's cell rang, and he clicked the button.

"Yes? Good. We've got her and we're on our way."

Gabe lifted Harper and carried her out of the cabin.

"I can walk," she insisted.

"I'm not letting go of you until we're safe in the helicopter. Santi, let's move it."

"Helicopter? What helicopter?"

He managed a grin. "Wait until you see. It belongs to this man here, Santi Vincent, our savior."

"He's certainly mine," she said in a shaky voice."

The moment they had lifted off the ground, Gabe contacted Stone.

"Mission accomplished on our end. What about you guys?"

"Wanted to make sure Harper was safe before we did anything, but Justice called to let us know they've had eyes on this asshole every minute. He's about to get a big surprise."

In the helo, Santi fished out a first aid kit that he handed to Gabe.

"Do something with her hands until we get her home."

Gabe nodded, turning to take Harper's bruised and scraped hands in his own. Then Santi banked the helicopter and headed in a new direction.

"Going to make sure Stone, Wade, and Justice grab this guy?" Gabe asked.

"We don't want him getting away. He's our only positive link to the people who did this."

"I know who did this," Harper blurted. "It had to be Culhane and Winslow. No one else had a reason to make me disappear."

"True," Gabe agreed. "Which is why we want to grab him and shake the truth out of him."

Harper shifted in her seat just behind Gabe.

"Mr. Vincent, I can't thank you enough for this. They stuck me in that place with a slop bucket, water, and a little packaged food. I was just trying to pry the bolt loose from the inside, at which I was having no success."

"It's an old line shack," he told her. "When we couldn't find a likely place for them to stash you in other areas we worked, I figured we should check the two ranches. They're big enough and spread out enough to hide someone."

"I'll never be able to thank you enough."

"Glad to help. But this is the guy you should thank." He pointed his thumb at Gabe. "He was like a bulldog."

"I wasn't giving up," Gabe told her. "I just found you. I couldn't lose you."

"So what happens after you grab this guy?"

"We bring in the sheriff and see if we can wrap up Culhane and Winslow in a big bow. It's about time they paid for their sins. And here we are."

As Santi descended, Harper looked through the windshield and saw a pickup on the highway skewed sideways and blocked by another helicopter. They landed a few feet away, and Harper could see Stone already talking on his phone. The man with him had her captor up against his pickup truck with his arms jerked behind him as he struggled against the zip ties being fastened around his wrists.

They'd removed his mask, and Harper thought he looked vaguely familiar, but she had no idea who he was.

"Sheriff's on his way." Stone shoved his phone back into his pocket. "I can tell you he's not happy about the situation. Two of the biggest landowners in the area and two of his biggest supporters? I promise you, his life is not about to get any easier."

"But he'll still do what's right," Santi said. "If he's smart, that is. Culhane has to realize he's been caught this time. All the politicians he's bought and paid for can't help him cover this up."

"He did it so he could have an unlimited wolf hunt." Harper's voice was edged with bitterness.

"If that's true, and I do believe it is, then the world of animal protectors and naturalists will be all over this. No hiding anymore." He looked at Gabe. "I'm happy to back up anything you say. Just holler."

"Thank you." Gabe shook the man's hand then turned to Harper. "Here comes the sheriff, and then I think it's time to get you home. I bet you could use a hot shower and a stiff drink."

"Yes, but I want to wait until I see this guy actually carted off. Then I'm ready to leave."

They watched as two SUVs with the sheriff's department logos painted on them pulled in behind the pickup truck. The man being held by Wade glared at everyone then spat on the road.

"I'll be home before dinner," he growled, "and you'll be looking for a new job, Sheriff. If, in fact, you can find one."

"Oh, I think you're wrong there," the sheriff said. "Kidnapping's one thing you can't get away with, no matter who you are."

"Prove it. You've got nothing."

The sheriff nodded at Harper. "I've got your

victim right here. If you want to carry the whole thing yourself, be my guest. You'll have plenty of time in prison to think about it."

The muscles in the man's face tightened as he realized the truth of what the sheriff said. He was cursing steadily as he was put in one of the sheriff's cars and they all drove away.

Gabe held a hand out to Santi Vincent. "Thank you more than you know for today. If you ever need anything, we're at your service."

"I'll take a tour of Wolf World, if that works. Never been there, and I'm very interested. Might even be interested in doing a little fundraising for it."

GABE SAW Harper's eyes light up.

"Any time you want to come over just call. I'm at your service."

"And now I think we need to get Harper home," Gabe said, as he helped her back into the chopper.

"I'm ready," she sighed. "I've had enough excitement for one day."

Gabe realized more than ever with the way she'd handled this the inner strength Harper had. If he hadn't been sure he was in love with her before, he knew it now.

CHAPTER 11

YOU'D HAVE THOUGHT all hell broke loose in Yellowstone and, in a way, it had. Harper's captor's name was Axel Redmond, and he worked for Ed Culhane. The rancher was beyond unhappy to get a visit from the sheriff in the middle of his big shindig. Stone Jacobs was also there, along with four deputies, just in case.

"What's he doing here?" Culhane growled to the sheriff, pointing to Stone. They had invaded the big party and hauled Ed off to his den. "Get him off my property."

"He's here with me. I wanted him to see every-thing was being done properly."

"I don't want him here. Get him off my property."

"He has every right to be here. He's the one who broke up your little kidnapping party."

"Kidnapping? Bullshit. Fucking bullshit. There must be some mistake here," Culhane insisted. "Get the hell out of here and off my property."

"No, sir. No mistake has been made. Not even a little," the sheriff assured him. "We know Axel Redmond is one of your hands who's been with you a long time. He's decided he doesn't want to do a stretch in prison by himself, and he can't get his story out fast enough. Maybe we can arrange for you two to be cellmates. Won't that be friendly."

"Whatever he's saying, he's a liar," Culhane insisted.

"A man who's been with you for twenty years? If he was, you'd have pitched him out long before this. He'll take you down with him."

"He's lying," Culhane insisted, "just like that bitch. You've got no proof."

"Only a man who's not going down by himself. Ed, I'm going to have to take you in. We can do this the easy way or the hard way. Up to you."

At that moment, Frank Winslow walked into the den with the deputy who'd been sent to fetch him from the tent where the party was still going strong.

"What's going on here? Sheriff, why are you here?"

The sheriff gave him the short version, and Winslow's face turned an unhealthy shade of red.

"That's a fucking lie."

"We've got the kidnapper in jail," the sheriff told him, "and he's singing loud and clear. No, I think the liars are you and your slimy friend here. Kidnapping a woman to have unlimited access to killing wolves? It doesn't get a lot worse than that."

Winslow opened his mouth to say something but thought better of whatever it was and took a different tack. "We have guests out there," he protested. "What am I supposed to tell them? How about if you leave Ed and me here until tomorrow so we can finish this shindig and then see them on the way?"

"What for?" the sheriff answered. "The hunt is canceled."

"I have the vet coming to collect semen for stud fees from my prize bull. Frank does, too."

The sheriff nodded. "Tell your foreman. He can handle it. You're gonna need that money for legal fees."

It still took some doing. Both Culhane and Winslow insisted on calling their attorneys, both of whom would have to fly in from Bozeman. Stone took great pleasure in heading to the tent with one of the deputies to announce the party was over.

"Better pack up your things," he told everyone.

They coerced two ranch hands into helping direct people gather their belongings and head to their vehicles. Most of them were staying in West Yellowstone, a number of them at John Jacobs' lodge, and they would have an escort while they took care of their business.

Meanwhile the sheriff and two deputies got ready to ferry Culhane and Winslow to the jail. Stone called Wolf World where all the men were still gathered waiting for news and asked for someone to pick him up in town. When Ridge showed up, he shook hands with the sheriff and thanked him for everything.

"No, thank *you*," the sheriff told him. "And Santi Vincent and all your guys. This would have been a disaster otherwise. Truth to tell, I'm glad to have a way to break the chokehold these guys have on the area. It's gone on long enough."

"My pleasure. I'm here if you need me for anything."

"I think this is a wakeup call for us to quit turning the other way where these rich assholes are concerned. I'm putting a call in to the governor, too. I doubt he'd want to be connected to someone associated with a kidnapping and break even more laws. Culhane may have inadvertently done us all a favor. Come on, dirtbags, let's get you the hell out of here."

The sheriff left, also, heading to his office to handle the dirtbags being stashed there.

Santi had flown Gabe and Harper back to Wolf

World where the rest of the team was waiting. Gabe had kept them in the loop via cell phone, but they wanted every detail.

"Scumbags," Ridge said. "I hope the judge throws the book at them.

"We'll make sure he does," John Jacobs assured them. "I guarantee it."

"They'll get my two cents' worth, also," Santi assured them.

"We can go over all the details later," Gabe broke in. "But right now, I think Harper wants to get cleaned up, and she definitely needs a drink and some rest."

"You're right," John said. "Let's get out of there and give these guys some privacy." He glanced at Gabe, who stood with his arm tightly around Harper. "I take it you won't be coming to the lodge anytime soon?" It was a statement, not a question.

"You got it." He frowned. "You all okay with that?"

John nodded. "I'd say Stone will be, too. Culhane and Winslow won't be the last ones to try and get around the hunting license laws. I'd say Harper is going to need full-time protection. If we need you for an assignment, we'll make arrangements to have someone here temporarily. There are plenty for former Special Forces around looking for pickup work."

"Thank you for everything," Harper told them. "Without you…" She shivered.

"Well, it's done and over with." He grinned at her. "Welcome to the team."

At last they were gone, two of the guys remaining to check the fence line for breaches and then make sure they were secure everywhere. They wouldn't leave until they were sure, but Gabe promised her that without Culhane and Winslow to give them orders, none of the ranch hands who had been shooting at her would venture close to Wolf World. He made sure everything in the office building was locked up tight then led Harper to the bathroom, where he turned on the shower. Gently, he peeled her clothes from her and tossed them to the side.

"I don't think you want to wear those again," he commented.

She shook her head. "Not even for a minute."

He stripped off his own clothes. When he was sure the shower was at the right temperature, he led her into the enclosure. Pouring body wash into his palm he soaped her from head to toe. There was nothing overtly sexual this time, just soothing strokes to relax her tense muscles. He worked her neck and shoulders before smoothing the lather down her hips and thighs.

Then he turned her around and did the same to her front. Even the strokes on her breasts and between her thighs were more soothing than arousing, although she had to admit her nerves were coming to life.

At last, he rinsed her off, led her out of the shower, and meticulously dried both of them. Then he led her into the bedroom, pulled back the covers on the bed, and eased her onto the sheets.

"I think we aren't finished with that massage yet," he told her, turning her onto her stomach. He began with her neck, kneading the taut muscles and working his way to her shoulders and arms.

"There's no chance these guys will get out of it, is there?" she asked, worried that with all their money Culhane and Winslow could buy their way to freedom.

"Not even a little. Santi has more money than both of them and a power circle of his own. He'll make sure of it."

She blew out a breath. "Thank god."

"Oh, god is definitely going to be on our side here," he promised her.

He worked her neck muscles and then moved his hands down her arms, over to her shoulders and slowly the length of her back. The shower had helped a lot, but this was so soothing, and Gabe's touch even more so. She felt herself finally relax. But when he kneaded the muscles of her buttocks, another kind of tension crept through her.

Maybe she could get him to move his hands in a different direction and…

Really, Harper. Thinking of sex after what you've just been through?

But it occurred to her she thought of sex almost every time she looked at the man. And when he slid his hands between her thighs and kneaded them with his palms, she was instantly hot with desire.

Holy hell!

"I think this might be the best way to get that nightmare out of your head." Gabe's voice was low and rough and thick with hunger and made her shiver with need.

"I think you might be right." *Yes! Yes! Yes!*

He rubbed gently back and forth on the lips of her sex, gradually easing his fingers inside her, but just a little bit. Not enough to bring her any kind of relief. She almost cried when he removed his hand and turned her over. But then he began with her shoulders again and moved to her breasts, gently squeezing them and sliding his thumbs back and forth across her nipples. When he stopped now and then to squeeze the now very hard buds, she sucked in her breath at the streaks of heat that flashed through her.

She had to bite her lips as he worked his way down her abdomen to the cease in her thighs.

When he cupped her mound and eased the tips of his thumbs into the top of the slit she couldn't swallow the moan that bubbled from her throat. He had such a magic touch. How had she been so lucky after her years of bad luck to find this incredible man and to have him feel the same for her that she did for him?

Nudging her thighs apart he knelt between them and stroked her damp slit, thumbs rubbing the slick surface up and down, up and down. She moaned again and pushed her pelvis toward his hands.

"More," she cried. "Please."

"Does this take away all images of Culhane and his asshole ranch hand??"

"Who's Culhane?" she cried. "What ranch hand?"

His laugh was low and rough and sexy.

"Exactly. He's nobody now."

He opened the lips of her sex wider, stroking his thumbs up and down until he stopped at her clit and pressed. A tiny orgasm burst from her, she lifted her hips, and a cry of need burst from her throat.

Gabe moved his hands to drape her legs over his thighs and pushed them wider apart. Then he slid his fingers into her sex, two of them, and moved them in and out, the aftershocks of the tiny releases fluttering against them. He added a third finger, pressed his thumb hard on her clit, and coaxed another small release from her.

"Enough with the teasing," he growled. "I only have so much control."

He reached into the nightstand drawer where he'd stashed condoms after the first time they'd made love and tore one off. Then he handed it to Harper.

"You do it," he told her in a raspy voice.

With shaking hands, she tore away the tinfoil then grabbed his very hard dick and rolled the rubber onto it. God! He was so hard and thick, even more than the last times, she thought. She rolled it slowly onto him, coaxing it slowly, feeling his cock get even harder and more swollen. When he was completely covered, she gave a little squeeze, eliciting a raspy indrawn breath.

"Jesus, Harper. Have a heart. I'm about ready to come right now."

"Then you'd better put this where it belongs."

She bent her legs, bracing herself with her feet on either side of his hips as he thrust slowly inside her waiting, welcoming sex. She knew the exact moment his control snapped. He braced himself on his hands and began driving into her with a hard, demanding rhythm. Her body responded, the inner walls of her sex gripping him hard. She dug her heels into the bed so she could keep up with his strokes, which came harder and faster.

They exploded together, the pulsing of his dick as intense as that of the walls of her sex. And when they came, it was like a burst of fireworks, shaking them and sending heat through their bodies. Her inner muscles clenched around him over and over, and she felt as if she was whirling through space.

At last, the intensity faded. Harper let her legs relax and fall to the side, and Gabe eased from her body with obvious reluctance.

"Back in a minute," he said, heading to the bathroom to dispose of the condom. Then he was back, sliding into bed next to her and pulling her warm, sweaty body next to his.

"That was just…" She blew out a breath, her body so weak she could barely move. "Wow!"

"It's always wow with us," he reminded her.

She nestled against him, wondering what came next but afraid to ask.

"Harper."

"Gabe."

They spoke at the same time.

"You first," he told her.

How do I say this?

"Now that the situation with Culhane is resolved," she began, "and I just have the normal challenges to deal with, will you…that is… Do you…I mean…"

He gave that rough laugh she'd come to love so much.

"I'm not going anywhere," he told her, "if that's what you want to know. I never thought my life could change so much in just a few days but, Harper, I don't want to walk away from this."

"Whew!" Relief washed through her. "That's good because I don't want you to."

"I'll still have assignments with the team, but I know Stone will be careful what they are and how often. And when I do, we'll still make sure you're protected because there will always be people after Wolf World."

"People who don't understand the importance," she agreed.

"And unless you have any objections, I'll be packing up my tent, storing it in the lean-to, and moving my gear inside." He gave her a squeeze. "So I can sleep next to your sexy body every night."

"I'd like that."

"Me, too." He paused. "You know, if there's a trial, you will probably have to testify. But I'll be with you every step of the way."

"I know you will. I couldn't do it without you."

"I wouldn't want you to," he assured her. "And I think the sheriff is going to pull in the ranch hands who took those shots at you, even though that may come to nothing, but he'll give it a shot."

Harper snuggled against Gabe, still wondering how her life had taken such a wonderful turn.

"I'm so glad you're the one Stone chose to give me protection."

"Me, too."

She lifted her face and they shared a long, emotional kiss. Life was looking better for her than it had in a long time.

Brotherhood Protectors Yellowstone World
Team Wolf
Guarding Harper - Desiree Holt
Guarding Hannah - Delilah Devlin
Guarding Eris - Reina Torres
Guarding Payton - Jen Talty
Guarding Leah - Regan Black

ABOUT DESIREE HOLT

USA Today best-selling and award-winning author **Desiree Holt** writes everything from romantic suspense and contemporary on a variety of heat levels up to erotic, a genre in which she is the oldest living author. She has been referred to by *USA Today* as the Nora Roberts of erotic romance, and is a winner of the EPIC E-Book Award, the Holt Medallion and a Romantic Times Reviewers Choice nominee. She has been featured on *CBS Sunday Morning* and in *The Village Voice, The Daily Beast, USA Today, The (London) Daily Mail, The New Delhi Times* and numerous other national and international publications.

Desiree loves to hear from readers.

If you are not already a member of my reader group, Desiree's Darlings, please come and join me. Every day is a party.
https://www.facebook.com/groups/
DesireesDarlings
Looking forward to "seeing" you there.

Desiree

www.facebook.com/desireeholtauthor
www.facebook.com/desiree01holt
Twitter @desireeholt
Pinterest: desiree02holt
Google: https://g.co/kgs/6vgLUu
www.desireeholt.com
www.desiremeonly.com

Follow Her On:

Amazon
https://www.amazon.com/Desiree-Holt/e/
B003LD2Q3M/ref=sr_tc_2_0?qid=1505488204&
sr=1-2-ent

BookBub
https://www.bookbub.com/search?search=
Desiree+Holt

Signup for her newsletter
http://eepurl.com/ce7DeE

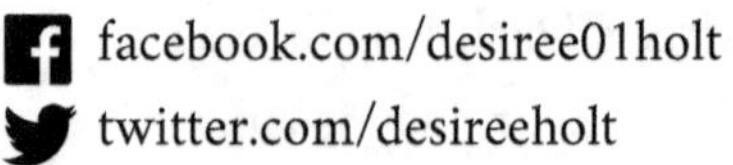

facebook.com/desiree01holt
twitter.com/desireeholt

Brotherhood Protectors Books by Desiree Holt

Hidden Danger

Prequels to Heroes Rising

Guarding Jenna

Unmasking Evil

Heroes Rising

Desperate Deception

Zero Hour

Fatal Secrets

The Hunt

Brotherhood Protectors Colorado

Team Trojan

Defending Sophie

Athena Project

Beck's Six

Brotherhood Protectors Yellowstone

Team Wolf

Guarding Harper

Montana D-Force (#3)

Cowboy D-Force (#4)

Montana Ranger (#5)

Montana Dog Soldier (#6)

Montana SEAL Daddy (#7)

Montana Ranger's Wedding Vow (#8)

Montana SEAL Undercover Daddy (#9)

Cape Cod SEAL Rescue (#10)

Montana SEAL Friendly Fire (#11)

Montana SEAL's Mail-Order Bride (#12)

SEAL Justice (#13)

Ranger Creed (#14)

Delta Force Rescue (#15)

Dog Days of Christmas (#16)

Montana Rescue (#17)

Montana Ranger Returns (#18)

ABOUT ELLE JAMES

ELLE JAMES also writing as MYLA JACKSON is a *New York Times* and *USA Today* Bestselling author of books including cowboys, intrigues and paranormal adventures that keep her readers on the edges of their seats. When she's not at her computer, she's traveling, snow skiing, boating, or riding her ATV, dreaming up new stories. Learn more about Elle James at www.ellejames.com

Website | Facebook | Twitter | GoodReads | Newsletter | BookBub | Amazon

Or visit her alter ego Myla Jackson at
mylajackson.com
Website | Facebook | Twitter | Newsletter

Follow Me!
www.ellejames.com
ellejamesauthor@gmail.com